White

Serpent

Castle

White Serpent Castle

Lensey Namioka

TUTTLE PUBLISHING
Boston • Rutland, Vermont • Tokyo

Originally published in 1976 by David McKay Company, Inc. Paperback edition first published in 2004 by Tuttle Publishing, an imprint of Periplus Editions (HK) Ltd., with editorial offices at 153 Milk Street, Boston, Massachusetts 02109.

Library of Congress Control Number 2004105506
ISBN 0-8048-3609-4

Distributed by

North America, Latin America & Europe
Tuttle Publishing
364 Innovation Drive
North Clarendon, VT 05759-9436
Tel: (802) 773-8930
Fax: (802) 773-6993
info@tuttlepublishing.com
www.tuttlepublishing.com

Asia Pacific
Berkeley Books Pte. Ltd.
130 Joo Seng Road
#06-01/03 Olivine Building
Singapore 368357
Tel: (65) 6280-1330
Fax: (65) 6280-6290
inquiries@periplus.com.sg
www.periplus.com

Japan
Tuttle Publishing
Yaekari Building, 3rd Floor
5-4-12 Ōsaki
Shinagawa-ku
Tokyo 141 0032
Tel: (03) 5437-0171
Fax: (03) 5437-0755
tuttle-sales@gol.com

First paperback edition
08 07 06 05 04   10 9 8 7 6 5 4 3 2 1

Design by Linda Carey
Printed in Canada

List of Characters

Zenta and Matsuzo, two ronin looking for work

Lord Okudaira, commander of a strategic castle in the north of Japan, recently dead

Chamberlain of the castle

Jihei, henchman of the chamberlain

Envoy, sent by Lord Okudaira's feudal overlord to mediate in the succession dispute

Saemon, chief retainer of the envoy

Ume, old woman serving Lady Tama

Young maid, serving Lady Tama

Lady Kaede, Lord Okudaira's second wife

Female warriors, serving Lady Kaede

Yoshiteru, Lord Okudaira's son by his second wife

Lady Tama, Lord Okudaira's daughter by his first wife

Shigeteru, Lord Okudaira's son by his first wife

Chapter 1

The two young samurai paused at a bend in the road. They stood for a moment and looked up at the length of white plastered wall which followed the contours of the hillside and lay as if about to uncoil. Seen from this angle, the castle looked like a huge white snake.

As the two travelers continued on their way, the main portion of the castle gradually came into view. The high point was the watchtower, soaring up into the sky like the head of a serpent poised to strike. The purpose of the castle was wholly military. Yet, seen in the late afternoon sun, the sprawling structure had an impressive grace and beauty.

"The name of the castle must come from its shape," said Matsuzo.

"The local people tell a different story," said Zenta. "They say that the name is from the legend of the White Serpent."

"You mean that ghost story they were telling back at the village?" said Matsuzo. He didn't want to admit he had been impressed by the story. According to the villagers, the daughter of a former lord of the region had thrown herself into the castle moat and changed into a monstrous white serpent. From that time on, the White Serpent Ghost emerged from its resting place in the moat whenever a crisis threatened.

"Apparently a report is around that the ghost has been seen at the castle recently," said Zenta.

Whether or not the report about the ghost was true, Matsuzo knew that the crisis was real enough. Lord Okudaira, the commander of the castle, had died a month ago and left his nine-year-old son as heir. These were troubled times. The control of such a strategic castle was of crucial importance. The nine-year-old boy would become the pawn of any unscrupulous man who seized power.

Already Zenta and Matsuzo had heard confusing rumors of a power struggle. According to one story, the chamberlain of the castle wished to make himself the legitimate successor of Lord Okudaira. To strengthen his position, he planned to force Lord Okudaira's daughter to marry him.

It was because of these rumors that the two men had come. They were *ronin*, unemployed samurai, going wherever there was promise of violence and confusion. In this struggle for the succession, they might find opportunities for work.

"What do you plan to do?" Matsuzo asked his companion. "Are we going to throw our support behind Lord Okudaira's young son?"

When Zenta didn't reply, Matsuzo said, "Surely you've decided? The boy is Lord Okudaira's only son and his official heir."

"It's true that the boy is Lord Okudaira's official heir," said Zenta. "But he is not the only son. He has an older brother."

Matsuzo stopped in his tracks and turned to look at his companion. "What? If there is an older son, why isn't he the successor, then?"

"The older son is missing," replied Zenta. "People around here haven't seen him for almost ten years."

There was a long silence. The two men walked on. Finally Matsuzo said, "How do you happen to know so much about Lord Okudaira's family?"

Zenta looked amused. "Since we were looking for work at the castle, I made it a point to learn as much as I could about the situation here. I'm surprised *you* didn't take the trouble to find out."

Under Zenta's quizzical gaze Matsuzo grew confused. "I suppose I did hear something about it," he muttered.

With a small shock he realized he knew nothing about his companion's family background. He had met Zenta a few months ago in a small village. The place was buzzing with talk about the five ronin who had routed a troop of bandits terrorizing the region. When Matsuzo saw Zenta, the leader of the five, he had been surprised to find him very spare of build, with no sign of any unusual strength. Matsuzo had been brought up on a diet of military romances, tales of heroism, and self-sacrifice. Seeing a chance to become the devoted follower of a great warrior, he approached Zenta and asked to be accepted as a pupil.

One by one, Zenta's other followers left, and Matsuzo soon discovered the reason why. A restlessness possessed Zenta like a disease. When they found well-paying work, he often decided to leave if he disliked the personality of his employer. On several occasions, they had to leave without pay, closely pursued by the fury of their recent master. The romantic tales failed to mention the unpleasant details in the life of a wandering ronin. Matsuzo learned to go for a week without a bath, to eat sweet potatoes when there was no money for rice.

But he stayed on with Zenta. Strangely, it was his love of the romantic tales that helped him to endure the hardships. If the famous hero Yoshitsune trudged many miles carrying luggage as a porter, then he could put up with a little discomfort, too.

As they walked, Matsuzo stole a glance at Zenta and saw that he showed no anxiety at all. Even with his clothes in tatters, the ronin didn't seem to care whether or not he would be hired at the castle. The only question was, would he accept Lord Okudaira's successor as his master?

The chamberlain could not possibly be an acceptable master, thought Matsuzo. The man was a usurper who was trying to gain his position by marrying his lord's daughter. The local people had been heard to mutter about the White Serpent Ghost whenever the chamberlain's marriage plan was mentioned, but when Matsuzo tried to question them about the connection, they would become evasive and refuse to meet his eye.

Only the superstitious villagers believed this ghost story, anyway, thought Matsuzo. He was much too intelligent to believe such nonsense. But he unconsciously quickened his steps, for night came very quickly in late October, and he felt an urge to reach the castle before it got dark.

The travelers now reached a thick grove of pine trees that formed a broad green belt around the castle. The trees served two purposes. They prevented the enemy from massing troops to attack the castle, and they screened the activities of the castle's defenders.

Once inside the shadows of the pine grove, Matsuzo felt the air grow cooler. There was a slight breeze which caused little rustling noises around them. Involuntarily he looked at his feet as he walked and occasionally peered at the underbrush.

Zenta's voice startled him. "Looking for the White Serpent Ghost? I heard the villagers say that the ghost is always accompanied by some eerie flute music. You'll get plenty of warning when it comes."

"I was afraid of tripping over a tree root," Matsuzo said sheepishly. He decided to distract himself by composing a little poetry. In the military romances, the heroes of old were always composing poetry. It was the mark of a true warrior to dash off a few elegant verses in the midst of danger.

The stealthy sounds of . . .

That didn't sound right. He tried again.

No birds sing
In the smothering darkness . . .

No, no, that wouldn't do at all. He abandoned poetry when he saw that the pine forest was thinning out and more light was coming through the trees. Suddenly his heart jumped into his throat as he caught sight of something shiny and white. Then he realized that he was looking at a stretch of water reflecting a white wall. They had reached the outer moat of the castle.

Rising from the moat was a gray wall built of boulders cunningly fitted together. This stone base was surmounted by a white plastered wall containing little round windows. The holes looked like eyes, and the slate tiles on the roof of the wall resembled the scales of a reptile.

Slowly the two ronin crossed the bridge spanning the moat. They did not stop at the huge metal studded gate, which was opened only for persons of rank, but instead turned to a small side door. Zenta gave the door two hard thumps.

After what seemed like a long time, they heard sounds of people moving about. There was another long silence. Zenta raised his hand and thumped the door again, more loudly this time.

"Who are you?" said a voice from a small round window just to their right. "What do you want?"

"My name is Konishi Zenta," replied the ronin. "My companion and I are seeking employment at the castle."

There were whispers and the sound of rapid footsteps. Somewhere in the distance another gate was being opened. Matsuzo had the feeling that the people inside were discussing them. It was true that the country had been in a state of civil war for nearly a hundred years, and a troop of strangers approaching the castle would naturally be treated with caution.

But he and Zenta were only two ronin looking for work. There was nothing in their appearances to cause alarm. Matsuzo flattered himself that he still looked like a well-bred young samurai of good family, and Zenta, as always, looked scruffy but utterly harmless. Then why should their arrival be causing so much nervous activity?

Without warning the side door opened quietly, and from the shadow of the door a voice spoke. "Please enter."

It seemed that they would be asked no further questions. As Matsuzo uneasily followed Zenta through the door, it immediately swung shut behind him with a small thud. The young ronin jumped and looked around quickly. He had just lost his last chance to leave.

The officer who had admitted them and the guards at the gate were all staring at the two arrivals with a strange intensity. Zenta, however, showed no sign of discomfort, but looked calmly about the courtyard until interrupted by the voice of the officer. "Please follow me," he said curtly to the two ronin.

The outer fortification of the castle consisted of a number of turrets and guard houses, connected by walls or by long, covered corridors. Samurai of lower rank had their quarters in this portion of the castle. The two newcomers and their escort threaded their way through this complex of buildings, making so many turns that Matsuzo soon lost his sense of direction. The mazelike effect was deliberate, for the planners of the castle had made sure that no direct approach to the center was possible.

As they passed, doors and windows slid open, and people leaned out to stare at them. Matsuzo began to find this excessive attention annoying. "One would think that we were

14

badgers in human clothing," he whispered to Zenta.

The officer turned at Matsuzo's whispering, and signaled to the escort to press closer.

After a few more turns, they found themselves in front of the inner moat, roughly a concentric circle within the outer moat. The walls of the innermost fortification rose steeply out of the water. Inside these walls were the residences of the castle's commander and samurai of high rank.

Matsuzo looked down into the stagnant water and wondered if this was the moat mentioned in the legend, where the girl had thrown herself. Was this where the monstrous white serpent rested? Suddenly he gasped and jumped back. He had seen something long and white stirring in the water.

One of the men in the escort laughed, and it was the first light note they had heard since entering the castle grounds. "You probably saw our giant albino carp. That fellow must be at least three feet long, and nobody knows just how old he is."

"Carp are carnivorous," remarked Zenta. "This moat would be an ideal place for throwing unwanted things . . . or people."

The face of the laughing guard darkened, and the party moved silently forward again. Crossing the bridge of the inner moat, they stopped in front of the gate which led to the heart of the castle.

Slowly, the heavy iron studded gate swung open. Waiting for them on the other side was a group of twenty armed men. It was an impressive reception for two penniless ronin.

At the head of the armed men stood a stoutish man of about forty, dressed with a showy richness which caused Matsuzo to wince. The stout man grinned broadly and surveyed the newcomers with satisfaction. "Ah, here you are at last. We have been expecting you."

Chapter 2

The stout man's words were heavy with menace, in spite of his smiling face. Hiding his alarm, Zenta bowed deeply to the welcoming party. "We are overwhelmed. But this reception can't be meant for two insignificant ronin. You must be expecting someone else."

The stout man smiled even more broadly. "I'm the chamberlain of this castle, in command since Lord Okudaira's death. I assure you that there is no mistake."

Zenta looked at the chamberlain and despised what he saw. This, according to rumor, was the ambitious schemer who was trying to marry his lord's daughter. The chamberlain's hands were soft and his body pudgy. He had the look of a man who ordered others to do the fighting.

Keeping a respectful expression on his face, Zenta said, "Let me announce our names, then. I am Konishi Zenta, and this is my traveling companion, Ishihara Matsuzo."

He nudged Matsuzo, who was staring with his mouth open. The young ronin gave a start and stepped forward, managing a creditable bow.

Zenta was aware of someone's hard stare on him. Standing next to the chamberlain was a tall, muscular samurai with heavy shoulders.

After studying Zenta closely, the samurai bent his head and spoke into the chamberlain's ear.

The chamberlain nodded and turned to the ronin. "Jihei here tells me that he has heard stories of Konishi Zenta. According to him, your appearance is not consistent with the stories."

"Really?" said Zenta. "I'm not sure whether I should feel flattered or insulted."

The chamberlain paid no attention to Zenta's remark. "Disarm these two men and take them into custody," he ordered the officer at the gate.

Zenta knew that people who met him for the first time were always skeptical of his identity. He remembered Matsuzo's open doubt and disappointment at their first meeting. But now the chamberlain's skepticism was dangerous. Zenta had just thought of a possible explanation for their ominous reception.

He had heard some talk that Lord Okudaira's older son was planning to return and claim his inheritance. He had not expected the chamberlain to take the rumor seriously, but if the chamberlain suspected that one of them was the missing older son, he would consider their arrival most inconvenient. Zenta didn't doubt that they would be taken somewhere to be quietly executed. It began to look as if coming to the castle was a serious mistake.

Zenta glanced quickly at Matsuzo and saw that the young ronin was waiting for a signal to draw his sword. Even if Matsuzo had not guessed the chamberlain's intention, he seemed to know how desperate their situation was. They had no chance of fighting their way out of the castle, but anything was better than going unresisting to their death.

Zenta had only one hope. He had been counting on finding forces opposed to the chamberlain within the castle. If he could delay his arrest and attract their attention, they might come to his aid.

The problem was that to draw one's sword in a feudal lord's castle, unless in self-defense or under orders, was a grave offense. Zenta decided that he had to provoke the chamberlain's men into becoming the aggressors.

When the officer approached to disarm him, Zenta took his short sword and threw it on the ground with the hilt towards the other man. This was a deadly insult, for the act said, "My contempt for you is such that I'm not afraid of putting my weapon in your hands."

The officer turned pale and his breath hissed. Determined to wipe out the insult, he drew his sword and rushed furiously at the ronin. His sword flashed up in a great arc and came down with an impressive swish. But it fell on air, for Zenta was no longer there.

Watching the officer struggling to regain his balance, Zenta laughed. "That was a breach of etiquette, you know. I've heard about cases of people who were ordered to commit hara-kiri for this."

Shifting his grip, the furious officer slashed again at his tormentor. The force of his swing nearly brought him to his knees, but Zenta had no trouble escaping the blow. He decided to play the furious officer the way a hunter might direct the charge of a wild boar. He maneuvered his position so that he was standing in front of the wooden gate. When the officer brought his sword down again, Zenta quickly ducked his head, and the sword was driven deeply into the wood.

Zenta looked around the courtyard. Had he succeeded in attracting the attention of the rest of the castle? He couldn't see any sign of additional activity. Very well, then, more drastic measures were necessary.

Looking over the rest of the chamberlain's men he said, "Is this officer a particularly bad example, or are you all as incompetent as he is?"

Meanwhile Matsuzo had finally realized what Zenta was trying to do. "Since the officer can't seem to get his sword out," he said loudly, "perhaps one of the other men could lend his. They don't have much use for their weapons here."

This taunt was too much for the self-control of the chamberlain's men. On all sides, swords flashed out as the men rushed forward without waiting for orders.

Zenta threw himself down to avoid an attack aimed at his head. Behind him another burly samurai rushed up with raised sword, but Matsuzo moved in to deflect the attack. The battle began.

When Zenta got to his feet, his right hand was holding his long sword, and his left hand was gripping the short sword which he had earlier thrown on the ground. Although the short sword was usually reserved for the ceremonial suicide, some samurai have developed a technique for using both swords at once.

The two ronin assumed a defensive position by placing themselves back-to-back. Surrounding them, the castle men did not immediately rush to attack. The samurai sword, razor sharp and exquisitely balanced, was not designed for constant hacking. Combatants tested each other with their eyes, not with physical contact, and the physical clashes, when they came, were savage and brief.

Suddenly two of the castle men lunged forward. Zenta's right hand swung down while his left hand flashed up and across. One man staggered back and the other one doubled up with pain. Matsuzo kicked him out of the way.

Once more the combatants froze in place. The courtyard was quiet except for the sound of rough breathing and someone's foot grating on sand.

Again there was an explosion of movement. One man aimed a cut at Matsuzo, who swerved to dodge the blow. The young ronin swung his sword in the stroke which he had learned from Zenta only two days earlier. His attacker stepped back, clutching his bleeding shoulder.

Darting a quick look at the blood, Zenta whispered, "Use the back edge of your sword, you fool! We don't want to kill anyone!"

"Maybe *we* don't, but *they* don't seem to feel the same reluctance," muttered Matsuzo.

The charges from the chamberlain's men were now coming faster. Zenta made a savage slashing attack, temporarily breaking the ring around them. When the encircling formed again, Matsuzo saw that Zenta had succeeded in shifting their position so that they were in front of the open gate.

Apparently the chamberlain realized it too. "Don't let them get away!" he screamed. "Close the gate!"

"With pleasure," answered Zenta. Stepping to one side, he swept the door into the faces of the four men advancing on him. There were resonant thumps of foreheads smacking against iron studs.

Matsuzo leaped for the other door. With a mighty push, the two ronin swept the door closed, pulling with it the officer whose sword was still stuck in the wood. At the same time the heavy door drove back three other attackers. The gate clanged shut with the three men left on the other side.

Breathing fast, Matsuzo spared a moment to flash a grin at Zenta before he whirled around to meet another furious attack. The number of attackers had been substantially reduced. Moreover, the two men now had the advantage of the gate protecting their backs. There was still the officer trying to free his sword from the gate, but he could not count as an active combatant.

By this time the chamberlain was jumping up and down in consternation, and even the heavyset Jihei was showing signs of wanting to join the fight.

"I think it's coming out," said the officer, who felt his sword loosen slightly from the door.

"Open the gate!" yelled the three men on the other side.

"Matsuzo, they want it open after all," said Zenta, and cleared a space.

With a sudden heave, Matsuzo pulled open the gate and quickly stepped aside. The three men pushing on the other side crashed into the attack of their own comrades.

The sudden jerk of the door jammed the officer's sword back into the wood.

In the confusion, Zenta and Matsuzo were again working their way to the open gate.

"Close the gate!" shouted the chamberlain.

"Can't you decide how you want it?" Matsuzo yelled back at him. In his excitement, he slipped on a patch of blood and crashed to the ground. Instantly two men were above him with raised swords. Zenta kicked the feet from under one man and drew the other away with a feint.

"At last! I got it out!" cried the officer, triumphantly waving his free sword. He swung it hard at Zenta, who quickly swerved. The sword sank back into the door.

In the tangle on the ground, Matsuzo found a hairy arm in his mouth. He bit. Struggling with the writhing heap above him, he thought, "Why is it that in all the great epic poems, fights were never so messy as this?"

Without warning, Matsuzo's opponents loosened their grip, and the young ronin realized that all sounds of fighting had stopped. In the background, an authoritative voice was speaking. Sitting up, Matsuzo looked around and found all the chamberlain's men crouched on the ground bowing to a figure high on the steps behind the chamberlain.

Chapter 3

"What is the meaning of this disgraceful exhibition?" demanded the new arrival.

Zenta saw that everyone, even the chamberlain, was bowing down to the ground. The new arrival was a man of very high rank indeed. Aside from Lord Okudaira's immediate family, who could possibly outrank the chamberlain?

"P-Pardon, m-my lord envoy," stammered the chamberlain. "This is all a dreadful mistake!"

Envoy from where, Zenta wondered. He risked a look and was slightly surprised to find that the envoy was a youngish man. His features were handsome but severe, with thick, lowering eyebrows. Two deep lines ran down either side of his nose to the corners of his lips, giving him a disdainful expression. From the deepness of the lines, Zenta guessed that the sneer was habitual.

The envoy frowned at the groveling chamberlain. "As the man in command of this castle, you are responsible for this disturbance. When the *daimyo* hears of this, he might judge you unfit for your position."

An envoy from the daimyo! The daimyo had been Lord Okudaira's feudal overlord, and the

25

presence of his envoy meant he was so concerned about the succession problem that he
found it necessary to send a mediator.

Zenta had finally succeeded in controlling
his breath, ragged from the fight. He raised his
head and said respectfully, "My lord envoy, I'm
afraid that I was the cause of this unseemly out-
break. I was seeking employment at this castle,
and there was a question of my qualifications.
A demonstration was needed."

In provoking the fight, he had accomplished his purpose and could afford to be
magnanimous. Now he wanted to save the men
of the castle from blame, and a low murmur of
relief from the men showed that they were
aware of this.

The envoy's brows rose. "This riot, then,
was merely to demonstrate your fitness?"

"I'm afraid that in our enthusiasm, some of
us got carried away a little," apologized Zenta.

The envoy's chief retainer, who had been
standing beside his master, now stepped forward. "If this man was just a ronin looking
for a job," he said to the chamberlain, "why
did you say that you expected him? You also
ordered your men to arrest him. Don't deny it.
I saw the whole thing."

The chamberlain stared helplessly, and
turned to the tall samurai next to him for inspiration. "We thought . . . that is . . . Jihei said he
got news that . . ."

Jihei interrupted smoothly. "We have been

getting reports of a notorious bandit who has been harassing this region. When these strangers appeared, it was only wise to take them into custody and check their identities."

"Yes, yes," agreed the chamberlain. "We were preparing a welcome for a terrible bandit!"

"And a very hearty welcome it was, too," said Zenta. "Do you go to all this trouble for every stranger who comes?"

The envoy was not ready to release his stern glance from the chamberlain. "Did the strangers draw their swords to resist? Was that how the fight started?"

Jihei stepped forward and answered for his master. "No, the officer who was escorting them lost his head and drew his sword first. Of course, he will answer for it."

"Are you perfectly satisfied now that these strangers are not the notorious bandits?" pursued the envoy.

A flash of pure hatred escaped from Jihei, but it was immediately suppressed. "Yes, my lord envoy. I am positive that they are not the bandits. This man is Konishi Zenta, just as he claimed. His particular style of fighting with two swords is very well known."

Zenta was convinced that Jihei and the chamberlain had not entirely given up their doubts about his identity. But in the envoy's hearing they couldn't very well say that they suspected him or Matsuzo of being Lord Okudaira's older son, since the envoy might seriously consider this son as a desirable candidate for the succession.

The envoy examined Zenta intently. "So you came to this castle to enter the chamberlain's service?"

"I was hoping to enter the service of Lord Okudaira's successor, whoever he turns out to be," replied Zenta. He looked calmly back at the searching eyes of the envoy. "Naturally I will wait for your decision on the question of succession."

After a moment the envoy said thoughtfully, "I may want to have a talk with you later."

He turned to the chamberlain and looked at him bleakly. "What has happened here this afternoon is no credit to the man in command of the castle. A report of this incident will certainly go back to my master the daimyo." With a contemptuous glance around, he signaled to his retinue and swept out of the courtyard.

The chamberlain scowled at the haughty back of the envoy and then turned to frown at his men. "What's the matter, you loiterers?" he barked. "Isn't there any work to do?"

Slowly the crowd dispersed, some of the men helping disabled friends to rise. More than one man looked at Zenta, who stood adjusting his swords in his sash. A limping samurai approached him respectfully. "We need you here, sir, to give us some lessons in swordsmanship."

Another man gingerly touched a painful lump

on his forehead. "I agree! I should like to see more of your two-sword technique."

Zenta grinned. "My first lesson on swordsmanship is a warning to avoid swinging gates."

Matsuzo straightened his clothes, feeling a certain amount of satisfaction. He had fought well and had used several newly acquired techniques. What would Zenta decide to do next? Now that there was no question of being taken into custody, they could leave the castle if they wished. For himself, he had even less desire to work for the upstart chamberlain now that he had seen the man. Unfortunately the chamberlain and his henchman Jihei seemed to be in complete control of the castle.

The chamberlain, who had been busily conferring with Jihei, now turned and beckoned to the two ronin. "We will forget about that little misunderstanding just now. My men acted hastily and got what they deserved. Now, I have positions open for warriors like you, and you will find the pay very generous. Waiting for the question of succession to be settled may take a long time, but if you enter *my* service, you can start drawing your pay immediately."

He glanced at Zenta's shabby brown kimono as he spoke. The afternoon's fighting had dealt a mortal blow to that long-suffering garment.

Matsuzo bridled at the chamberlain's condescending tone, but Zenta did not seem offended at all. "A bath, a clean kimono, and some food would be very welcome," he confessed.

The chamberlain nodded without seeming to notice that Zenta had not committed himself. He gave a sign of dismissal and turned away in a swirl of colors. With the departure of his gorgeous costume, the whole courtyard seemed quieter.

The two ronin found Jihei in front of them. "Come with me. I will show you to your quarters."

"I hope they're not the ones which you had prepared for the bandits?" asked Matsuzo, trying to imitate Zenta's ironical tone.

Jihei gave a short laugh, but his eyes were cold. "This way, gentlemen," he said.

When Jihei took them to a door in the base of the watchtower, Matsuzo asked in surprise, "Then you're not going to put us in the outer fortress?"

"The chamberlain's opinion of you is so high that he is putting you in the inner fortress together with officers of the household," replied Jihei. The words were flattering, but there was a hint of grimness in Jihei's voice which Matsuzo did not like.

The three men mounted some stairs and soon found themselves on the ground floor of the central building which formed the base of the watchtower. The rooms here were airy and light, but rather bare. In the older and more primitive castles, the commander sometimes had his living quarters in the watchtower building, but Lord Okudaira had more luxurious quarters constructed for his household.

Leaving the watchtower building, Jihei swiftly led the two ronin along a series of narrow hallways, bewildering in their constant twists and turns. Matsuzo had to hurry to keep up with Jihei's long strides. "Strangers to this castle could be lost for days here," he panted.

"The mazelike effect is our best defense," said Jihei with satisfaction. "Even if attackers were to get past the outer fortress and reach this building, they would wander around aimlessly and find themselves ambushed by our men at every turn."

"With an impregnable castle like this, it seems strange that your chamberlain should be so nervous," said Zenta. "Forgive me if I sound impertinent, but I got the impression that everyone here is on edge."

"You are thinking of those fools who started the fight by the gate," said Jihei. "They were just some hotheads who needed a lesson."

"Perhaps people here are jumpy because of the White Serpent Ghost," Matsuzo put in.

Jihei looked annoyed. "How did you hear about the ghost?"

"Well, it's the chief topic of conversation in the region," said Matsuzo. "Everybody here is talking about the death of Lord Okudaira and the White Serpent Ghost."

Jihei's lips curled contemptuously. "Those idle gossipers! They make up these stories in order to attract travelers to their business."

"You mean the chamberlain's intended marriage to Lord Okudaira's daughter is only gossip?" asked Matsuzo.

"Those peasants are talking about the chamberlain's intention to marry Lady Tama?" cried Jihei. "The incredible insolence! We'll soon put a stop to this idle talk!"

"I think the villagers really believed the stories," said Matsuzo. "We got such a vivid description of the white serpent slithering down the hall, and of the ghostly flute music."

"Ha! Now I know who is responsible for these stories!" said Jihei. "It must be Lady Tama's servant Ume! That old woman is either in her second childhood or sleepwalking. She claimed to have seen a dim white shape one night, and she managed to get the whole household upset."

"What about the ghostly music, then?" asked Matsuzo.

Jihei gave a sigh of sorely tried patience. "There are several ladies in the castle who can play the flute. One of them may have been practicing late at night. As for the long slithering thing, those silly maids were probably chasing each other's sashes!"

In spite of Jihei's vigorous denials, Matsuzo was reluctant to abandon the serpent ghost and eerie flute music. They made such good subjects for poetry.

Suddenly Zenta said, "Speaking of foolish fancies, for a moment I thought that your chamberlain mistook one of us for Lord Okudaira's missing older son. Ridiculous idea, isn't it?"

Jihei stopped. He turned around slowly and looked hard at the ronin. "What do you know about Shigeteru?"

"Shigeteru—is that his name?" said Zenta. "I'm a stranger to this region, and I can't tell you anything. Do you know the cause of his disappearance?"

In the slanting light from a small window, Jihei's expression was hard to read. "Ten years ago, a serious break took place between Shigeteru and his father. I had not yet been hired here, but I heard that it happened during a battle in which Lord Okudaira's sudden retreat caused some men to be stranded and killed. One of those killed was a close friend of Shigeteru. In his grief he spoke wildly and dared to accuse his father of cowardice. For such disrespect to his father he could have been sentenced to commit hara-kiri. But because of his extreme youth, he was spared and instead sentenced to exile."

"You don't know what happened to him afterwards?"

"There were reports that he was leading a band of ronin in a distant province," said Jihei.

"In that case he can't be the cause of the tension here at the castle," said Matsuzo.

Jihei took a moment to answer. "We have heard rumors that Shigeteru has returned to this region. He must have received news

33

of his father's death and is looking for an opportunity to take over the castle."

Zenta looked dubious. "You don't seriously expect Shigeteru to mount an assault on this castle with his band of ronin, do you?"

"We are not afraid of an attack from the outside," said Jihei grimly. "We are watching for someone trying to start an insurrection from within the castle."

"I see," mused Zenta. "I did notice when we passed through that most of the outer garrison seemed to have been moved to the inner fortress." He turned and looked searchingly at Jihei. "I have heard that if Shigeteru were to appear, nobody at the castle would recognize him. Is this true?"

There was no doubt that Jihei found the question annoying. "It's true that the chamberlain took office after Shigeteru's exile, and most of the men here are new. But how did you hear?"

"It's common knowledge that the chamberlain has been sending away the old retainers to outlying forts and replacing them with men loyal to him," replied Zenta. "News like that spreads quickly among ronin who are looking for work."

"I heard that he was doing this even before Lord Okudaira's death," said Matsuzo. "He started placing his own men in the castle as soon as his master fell ill."

Zenta smiled maliciously at Jihei. "There-

34

fore in his haste to fill the castle with men of his own choice, the chamberlain is left with no one who can recognize Shigeteru. That would explain why he pounces suspiciously on every stranger who comes knocking at the gate."

Jihei looked furious. "We can always call in a few of the old retainers from outlying forts and have them identify Shigeteru!"

"But you can't rely on help from the old retainers," Zenta pointed out. "They might be loyal to Shigeteru, and actually help him in his plan to take over the castle."

Jihei started violently at the ronin's last words. Then he collected himself and said curtly, "I suggest that you watch your tongue if you wish to stay in the chamberlain's service." He stopped before the room assigned to the two newcomers and swept open the sliding door with an angry crash.

Waiting for them inside the room was an old woman. At the sight of her Jihei's anger increased further. "Ume! What do you think you are doing here?" he demanded.

Chapter 4

The old woman addressed as Ume bowed to the floor. When she lifted her head, she showed a face so wrinkled that the two slits of her eyes could hardly be seen. Her voice was low and very hoarse. "My mistress, like everyone else in the castle, has heard details of the fight in the courtyard. She is very happy that such valiant warriors are to be in our service, and she sent me to attend to their needs."

"Lady Tama has nothing to do with hiring new retainers!" said Jihei angrily. "Get out and go about your lady's service!"

A man put his head in the door. "Jihei, the chamberlain wants you immediately."

"Meddlesome old fool," muttered Jihei, throwing a furious look at the old woman as he left.

Ume went to the door and peered cautiously up and down the corridor. When Jihei's footsteps died away, she turned back and closed the door.

From the window of the room Matsuzo could see down into the innermost courtyard. In this enclosure were the buildings that accommodated the castle's commander, his family, and other persons of high rank. Unlike the more austere quarters of the warriors, these buildings were luxurious and opened into beautifully landscaped gardens. The court-yard presented a peaceful scene, with the security that came from the protection of two encircling fortresses and moats.

Matsuzo turned from the window and prowled about the room, peeking into the cupboards and testing the thickness of the folded quilts inside them. These quilts would be unfolded and spread out later to become their beds. He was glad to see that the quilts were padded with silk floss. They would be very light and warm, unlike the stiffer cotton padded quilts that he had been sleeping on recently.

He finally loosed his clothing, pulled out a big cushion and sat down with a satisfied grunt. It had been a strenuous afternoon.

He saw that Zenta and Ume were silently studying each other. Ume looked slightly dis-appointed, and Matsuzo knew that she had the usual reaction of people seeing Zenta for the first time. Most of them, hearing about his exploits, expected a ferocious giant, not this harmless looking young samurai whose build was slender rather than muscular.

Finally the old woman broke the silence. "My lady wished to make sure that you have everything you desire."

"That is most gracious of Lady Tama," said Zenta politely.

Ume's small bright eyes stared hard at the ronin. Then she broke out into an ingratiating smile. "Serving Lady Tama can be very pleasant as well as profitable. She has many attendants who are beautiful and accomplished."

Zenta looked amused. "What an irresistible prospect! But at the moment, all you have to do is offer me food. I don't remember when my last meal was."

"I have already ordered food to be brought to you," said Ume impatiently. "What my lady wants to know is whether you will enter *her* service, instead of the chamberlain's."

Zenta's face showed surprise. "In what way can a ronin like me serve your lady? As Jihei said just now, it is not Lady Tama's business to hire samurai for the castle."

"Have you sworn allegiance to the chamberlain then?" demanded the old woman.

"I believe I will put off my allegiance until the envoy gives his decision on the succession."

"My lady says that the envoy's decision depends largely on who is in actual command here," said Ume. "Our daimyo wants most of all a warrior as commander of this castle, and he is likely to accept anyone who is strong enough to seize control here, provided he has a legitimate claim."

This time Zenta's surprise looked more genuine. "Your mistress has the mind of a strategist! It's a pity that the daimyo can't appoint a woman, because Lady Tama appears well qualified to succeed her father."

Ignoring this remark, Ume continued. "With

the help of your sword, we should be able to take the control away from the chamberlain and win the support of his men."

Matsuzo listened openmouthed with astonishment. Lady Tama sounded like a formidable girl. If the chamberlain succeeded in forcing her into marriage, he would find life quite harrowing, aside from any additional attentions he might receive from the White Serpent Ghost.

Even Zenta sat up upon hearing the old woman's words. "I have a few objections to your ambitious plan," he said. "First, Jihei seems like a very competent officer, and I don't think his men will come running to me just because of my showy footwork in the courtyard. Secondly, you have not mentioned Lord Okudaira's younger son. I have heard that he is the designated heir."

"Designated heir indeed!" sneered Ume. "Lord Yoshiteru is only nine years old. He is hardly the seasoned warrior that the envoy wants for his master."

"Yoshiteru will have military advisors, and his mother can guide him in other matters," said Zenta. "Situations like this are not unknown in the history of our country."

"His mother, Lady Kaede, is Lord Okudaira's second wife, and a noblewoman from Miyako," said Ume. "Women like that are soft, not like Lady Tama, who has been brought up in the military tradition. No, what we need is an heir who is of age."

After a rather tense silence, Matsuzo spoke first. "You are referring to the older son, Shigeteru, aren't you? Lady Tama wants to see him as lord of this castle?"

Before Ume could answer, Zenta said, "You may be one of the few people here who has seen Shigeteru. The chamberlain sent away most of the older retainers, but you have been here from the time of Lord Okudaira's first wife, haven't you?"

Ume nodded. "Yes, but since my service was in the women's quarters, I caught only a few glimpses of Lord Shigeteru. Poor lad, he had not quite finished growing when he left, and the hair over his forehead was still cut short in the style of early youth. Of course I won't recognize him if I see him now."

In spite of her denial, she sounded curiously smug and satisfied. Suddenly Matsuzo was convinced that she was lying and that she was confident she would recognize Shigeteru. Her air of suppressed excitement might mean that Shigeteru was actually here in the castle and she had already seen him!

If Zenta suspected the same, he gave no sign. "Are you expecting me to start an uprising on Shigeteru's behalf? If so, I shall have to disappoint you. Your plan sounds foolhardy and I want nothing to do with it."

In Ume's wrinkled face her small eyes flashed menacingly, but all she said was, "Of course you have only just arrived, sir, and don't wish to commit yourself yet. We shall see." She moved to the door. "I'll have food sent and order some maids to prepare a bath for you."

Zenta called her back. "Just a moment. There is something else I want to ask you. We heard that you have seen the White Serpent Ghost. Can you describe it for me?"

The old woman looked wary. "It's not easy to describe something not of this earth. All I can say is that I saw a long white thing, faintly shimmering as it crawled along. I also heard strange flute music in the background during the appearance of the ghost."

She gave a shudder which struck Matsuzo as false. He exchanged a smile with Zenta, and at that the old woman stiffened. "I was not the only person to see the ghost!" she said angrily. "Since that first night many other people have both seen the ghost and heard the music!"

"Jihei said it was probably a woman's sash that you saw," said Matsuzo.

"I know what a woman's sash looks like! That monstrous thing which I saw was thick and fleshy! Of course, a henchman of the chamberlain would talk like that."

"Why a henchman of the chamberlain particularly?" asked Zenta.

Ume smiled grimly. "Because the ghost is a warning of what would happen to the chamberlain if he tried to marry Lady Tama."

"This is what some of the villagers said, but

nobody would give me a good explanation," complained Matsuzo. "What exactly is the story of the White Serpent Ghost?"

"Ah, you've asked the right person," said Ume. She closed her eyes and cleared her throat for launching into the story.

"A hundred and twenty years ago, the lord of this region had an only child, a daughter who was surpassingly fair. Her skin was white and sparkled like new snow. Not only was she beautiful, but she was also a most talented musician. The lord could not find a husband who was worthy of his daughter's hand."

Ume rolled off the narrative smoothly, as if she had told it many times. Matsuzo suspected that it was Lady Tama's favorite bedtime story.

"It happened that the lord died suddenly after a short illness. A dispute followed about who should be his successor. One of the strongest contestants was a cousin who was only a distant relative. But he was a powerful man with many supporters, and he decided to strengthen his position further by marrying the daughter. However, she was still beside herself with grief for her father, and she hated this cruel, ugly suitor. Nevertheless, preparations for the marriage went on despite her protests.

"Then on the night before the wedding, she sent away her attendants and shut herself in her room. As time passed, the attendants began to worry, and they decided to look in. They found the room empty. Her clothes were in a heap on the floor, but the girl had disappeared. It was thought at first that the desperate girl had thrown herself into the moat, but several witnesses saw something very long and white crawl away from the moat into the trees. They claimed that it looked like a huge white snake."

Matsuzo shifted his position uneasily. He knew it was only a story, but told in Ume's low, hoarse voice, it made uncomfortable hearing.

"The ghost was seen in the castle soon afterwards," Ume went on. "It was always a long, white slithering shape accompanied by eerie flute music. People remembered that the daughter had been an accomplished player of the horizontal flute. As for the cruel suitor, his fate was a terrible one. He began to feel icy things crawling across his neck at night, and he was dead within a month. Some say he died of fright, some say he was strangled."

Matsuzo's hand involuntarily went to his throat and he swallowed. He glanced at Zenta and saw that he was listening to the story with a faint smile.

"Since that time," continued the old woman, "the ghost has appeared several times in this region. In each case, it was at a time when a girl was forced into marriage soon after the death of her father. You can see an obvious parallel between the old legend and Lady Tama's situation. That's why the appearance of the ghost now is enough to frighten the chamberlain."

"And it is clear why the appearance of the ghost must be very welcome to Lady Tama," remarked Zenta.

"Are there many ladies here who play the bamboo flute?" asked Matsuzo with a grin, anxious to prove that the ghost story had not frightened him in the least. "Lady Tama is probably an expert player at this instrument."

Ume looked furious. "So! You dare to accuse us of arranging a fake ghost! Just wait, you skeptics. There are horrible stories about people who refuse to believe in ghosts!"

Zenta laughed. "When I feel icy things on my neck, my last doubt will vanish!"

The old woman's face suddenly became blank. She bowed without a word, and sliding open the door she quietly left the room.

Chapter 5

Zenta could see that his companion had a question on the tip of his tongue. As soon as the door closed behind the old woman, Matsuzo asked, "Do you think that Shigeteru will try to get in touch with Ume?"

"Why does everyone assume that Shigeteru and his men are coming?" said Zenta.

"Well, the chamberlain and Jihei seemed to expect his coming," said Matsuzo. "Perhaps they have some definite news."

"Shigeteru would be a stupid fool to come here and attempt to take over the castle by force," said Zenta. "He would be an even greater fool to reveal his identity to that gossipy old woman."

"He might not have any choice about revealing his identity," Matsuzo pointed out. "I think she would recognize him."

"I doubt it," said Zenta. "You heard what Ume said: Shigeteru was only a boy when he left. Ten years, at his stage of growth, can change his looks completely."

"I still think Ume knows something," insisted Matsuzo.

Zenta didn't bother to answer. Ume was stupid and thought herself cunning, a disastrous combination in a conspirator. He wanted no part of her dangerous plots. Taking out his two swords, he sat down on a straw cushion and began a minute examination of the blades. Then from a little pouch attached to his sash he took out a small jar of oil and some rags. With these he polished his swords, his hands caressing the beautiful grain of the blades.

It had been said that a samurai's sword was his soul. For Zenta, his swords were also his only constant companions in his lonely, wandering life. They had been given to him by a grateful warlord. For a while his future at the court of this warlord had looked bright, but he had left that job, just as he had left so many other promising jobs.

Zenta glanced at Matsuzo and wondered how long the young ronin would be able to stand their life of restlessness and near starvation. Even worse was the occasional humiliation, such as when they had to ask for lodgings at farm houses because there was no money for an inn.

"Would you like to stay at this castle permanently?" Zenta asked his companion.

Matsuzo looked wistful. "This is a strong castle, from what I've seen of it so far. Are you planning to stay on after the succession dispute is settled?"

For an instant Zenta was gripped by a longing so intense that it was suffocating. Then their door slid open.

A pretty maid with roguish eyes poked her

head in and said, "Your bath is ready, gentlemen."

"Ah, at last!" said Matsuzo. "I was afraid that we had been forgotten."

The two men followed the maid down some stairs. More than once she glanced back coyly at them, and her expression said plainly that she was one of the advantages they could expect if they entered Lady Tama's service.

They stepped out of a door and into a quiet courtyard. The stars were already out and the air was cold.

"This way, please," directed the little maid.

The bathhouse was a small wooden building consisting of a dressing room and a washing room. The floor of the washing room was of widely spaced slats, so that water could run off when the bather squatted on it to scrub and rinse. The tall square tub for soaking was made of fragrant cypress. It was brimming with hot water which gave off clouds of steam, a most welcome sight on this chilly night.

"Do you have everything you need, gentlemen?" asked the little maid. "I shall be back soon with some clean clothes." With a bow, she left the dressing room.

"Please be first," said Matsuzo.

Zenta lost no time in shrugging out of his torn clothes and stepping down into the washing room. First he splashed himself with a bucket and then, using a sponge made of gourd fiber, he began to scrub away a week's accumulation of grime. Then he rinsed himself and, thoroughly cleansed, climbed into the steaming tub for a soak. He sat down gingerly until he was up to his neck in the scalding water, which was heated to the limit of endurance by a small fire beneath the tub. "Ah . . ." he sighed, and closed his eyes in bliss. It had been a long time since he had last enjoyed a private bath like this, a pleasant change from public baths where a dozen or more people shared a tub.

In the dressing room Matsuzo squatted in front of a large mirror and tried to retie his topknot neatly. The little maid who had showed them to the bath was charming, and Matsuzo hoped that she would return in time to scrub his back. He thought it likely that she would serve dinner to them later. Her cheeks dimpled delightfully when she smiled, and he intended to find out if she would be free after dinner.

The thought of dinner made Matsuzo very hungry, and he was glad when Zenta called out that he was nearly through with the soaking. Undressing promptly, Matsuzo stepped down into the washing room and prepared to scrub himself. He was just in time to see the window behind Zenta opening.

Before Matsuzo had time to call out a warning, Zenta's head jerked up. With a tremendous splash he bounded out of the tub and rushed out of the bathhouse.

Drenched and bewildered, Matsuzo blinked

the water from his eyes and followed his companion. Guided by the sound of crackling shrubbery, he made his way to the back of the building. He found Zenta standing at the open window which had been directly behind the bathtub.

"What happened?" he asked.

Zenta motioned Matsuzo to be silent. He listened intently and peered all around. There was not a sound. "When I was in the tub just now, I felt something icy go down the back of my neck," he said slowly.

At these words, Matsuzo could almost feel ice on his own back. His teeth began to chatter.

Footsteps approached, and both men whirled around. They saw two shadowy figures walk up to the bathhouse. In the light from the open window, Matsuzo recognized Ume and the little maid.

The saucy little maid was holding a pile of clothes in her arms, and at the sight of the shivering, naked men, she broke into giggles.

Ume kept a straight face and inquired politely, "Was everything quite satisfactory in the bathhouse, gentlemen?"

Zenta stared intently at the old woman. Suddenly he threw back his head and started to laugh. "Everything was nice, except that I felt a draft behind my back. It seemed that one of the windows in the washing room was not securely fastened."

For an instant Ume's wrinkled face showed

grudging respect. "How careless of me!" she exclaimed. "I shall see that it doesn't happen again. And now we must help you to finish your bath before you get chilled. Your dinner is already prepared and will be brought to your room shortly."

"That will not be necessary," said the voice of Jihei. "My master requests the company of these two gentlemen at dinner tonight."

In spite of his size, he had moved very quietly and they had not heard his approach. If he saw anything strange about the two ronin standing naked in the cold night air, he kept his thoughts to himself. He turned to the women and said curtly, "You are not needed here. Take yourselves off immediately."

As the three men walked back to the entrance of the bathhouse, Jihei said, "When I returned to your room, I discovered that you had already left for the bathhouse. That meddling old hag certainly lost no time trying to recruit you. What did she offer?"

"Offer?" asked Zenta innocently. "Why, she offered us a bath."

Jihei looked sourly for a moment at the ronin without speaking. Then he turned abruptly and walked down the path. "You will have to hurry if you don't want to be late for the dinner," he said over his shoulder.

Chapter 6

The two ronin were in time to join the last of the dinner guests assembled and waiting to file into the dining hall. They were surprised to learn that they would be dining with the envoy and some of his men. It was an unexpected honor for the two ronin.

Zenta was usually very careless of his appearance, and Matsuzo was relieved that for this occasion he had taken the trouble to look almost presentable. The two men were wearing the kimonos brought by the little maid, and as Matsuzo settled the sleeves of his, he could still smell the faint perfume of the storehouse incense.

At first glance Matsuzo found the huge dining hall rather austere. The wooden floor was bare and polished to a mirror smoothness. Seating for the guests consisted of flat round cushions of braided rice straw. But Matsuzo soon detected signs of elegance. The tall candlesticks were of beautifully chased bronze, and one wall of the room was almost completely covered by a painting of a pine tree. The picture dominated the room with its vivid green and gold. Matsuzo knew enough about art to tell that the painting was the work of a master. He suspected the influence of Lord Okudaira's second wife in the furnishings. A lady from the capital city, used to elegance and sophistication, would want to soften the austerity of a feudal lord's castle.

The diners sat down along three sides of the room, with the daimyo's envoy at the place of honor in front of the painting. By the somber richness of his kimono, the envoy made the chamberlain's bright colors look cheap. Even for this social occasion, the envoy's face did not relax from its rigid hauteur. Three of his retainers were at the dinner, and they behaved with equal aloofness.

An individual tray of food was set on the floor in front of each diner, and the first course began. Servants scurried around diligently filling saké cups, but in spite of their efforts, the party showed no signs of becoming a success.

Looking over the dinner guests, Matsuzo thought that they formed a rather ill-assorted company. He glanced from the aristocratic envoy to the fawning chamberlain, who was seated next to the guest of honor. Below him was Jihei, holding a ridiculously delicate china wine cup in his huge, powerful hands.

Sitting beside Jihei was the envoy's chief retainer, a samurai called Saemon. Matsuzo remembered him as the man who had spoken to the chamberlain in the courtyard that afternoon. Saemon had a pleasant face, clever-looking and humorous. Although not powerfully built like Jihei, he gave the impression of wiry strength. For some reason Matsuzo suspected that Saemon was more intelligent than his master the envoy. Perhaps it was the way the envoy frequently looked at his retainer, as if for guidance.

Matsuzo's eyes finally went back to Zenta, who was hunched over his tray wholly occupied with food. In fact his concentration on food was almost embarrassing to see.

Meanwhile the chamberlain was struggling to make pleasant conversation with his unresponsive guest of honor. "Did you have good weather on your way up? It can get quite blustery at this time of the year."

"I didn't notice the weather, since I was traveling on an important mission," answered the envoy coldly.

It was heavy going, but the chamberlain was not easily discouraged. "I used to make the trip to the daimyo's capital quite often when I was a youth. In recent years, of course, my duties at the castle have prevented me from traveling. But I still remember one particularly bad river that had to be forded. Do you know the one I mean?"

"An account of your youthful adventures is no doubt of overwhelming interest to *some* of the people in this room," said the envoy, openly yawning.

The chamberlain flushed. Turning to scowl at the serving girl holding the wine jar behind him, he said, "Stop dawdling and hurry up with that saké! Who was responsible for your training, anyway?"

"Since the girl was probably trained in Lord Okudaira's household," said the envoy acidly, "perhaps it's a good thing that your master is not alive to hear your criticism."

That silenced the chamberlain, and for the next few minutes, conversation in the dining hall languished. Then the chamberlain emptied three cups of saké in rapid succession and picked up the courage to try again. He launched into a description of the castle, and he finally seemed to have found a topic that interested his guests.

Matsuzo saw that Saemon's eyes were bright with interest as he listened to the chamberlain's talk on the castle's fortification, and even the envoy's sneer was less pronounced. Only Zenta, busily eating, paid no attention.

"And by the time the stone base for the outer wall was completed," said the chamberlain, "our castle became one of the most strongly fortified in this part of the country." He turned to Zenta. "You have traveled widely, I'm told, and you must have seen a great deal. What do you think of it?"

"What?" Zenta's reply was muffled. He hurriedly swallowed some fish and held out his wine cup to the waiting servant. "I think that serving it raw with chopped herbs and soy sauce is an excellent way of preparing this fish, but I also like it rubbed with coarse salt and broiled."

He seemed not to notice the smiles that greeted his remark, and he added, "By the way, it seems ungrateful to mention this after receiving all this lavish hospitality, but when I was taking a bath this evening, I felt something icy crawl down my neck. It was a most peculiar sensation. Perhaps you should have the bathrooms here checked for pests?"

In the silence that followed, Matsuzo heard a faint plop. A piece of raw fish had fallen from the chamberlain's nervous hand into his wine cup.

The envoy was the first to speak. "Since I arrived at this castle, there have been disturbances in the night. My retainer Saemon made inquiries, and he told me that people here claim the disturbances were caused by something called the White Serpent . . ."

Jihei broke in. "That's just pure feminine hysteria!"

"You mean that I was suffering from feminine hysteria?" asked Zenta gently.

"Of course, I didn't mean you," said Jihei impatiently. "I was referring to those women who said they saw a long white thing and heard ghostly music."

"Some of the samurai here say that they have heard the ghostly music, too," said Saemon.

"One of the women could be deliberately playing a trick on us," growled Jihei.

"But if it's just a woman's trick, why can't you find out how she did it and stop her?" asked Zenta.

"It's not as easy as you think!" said Jihei angrily. "Most of the disturbances took place in the women's quarters, and we're not supposed to go there. But the next time there is an outcry about the ghost, I promise that we will make a very thorough search into every corner of the castle, even if it does take us into the women's quarters!"

"Are you saying that some woman in this castle is pretending to be the ghost?" asked the envoy. "What can be her reason for doing this?"

The chamberlain said hurriedly, "Jihei only means that he is a realist and is not ready to believe in anything without solid proof."

Turning to Jihei he said, "But by its very nature, it's impossible to get solid proof of a ghost. These old legends are never completely without foundation, you know. We shouldn't offend the spirits by too much skepticism."

"Nevertheless we should search carefully for traces of human handiwork behind the ghost," insisted Jihei.

As the trays for the first course were removed and the second course brought in, a serving woman came in, bowed and spoke to the chamberlain in a low voice.

The chamberlain gave a start of surprise and smiled happily. "We are indeed fortunate tonight," he announced. "Lady Kaede wishes to honor our distinguished guests, and she is having some of the castle's prized saké brought out to be served."

A double sliding door opened and Lady Kaede, Lord Okudaira's widow, entered the room. She was followed by a procession of serving girls holding trays with heated bottles of saké.

Lady Kaede looked so young that Matsuzo found it hard to believe she had a nine-year-old son. He remembered Ume saying that Lady Kaede was from one of the noble families of Miyako, and he could imagine the generations of inbreeding that went into producing her fine bones. Transplanted from the milder Miyako air, she looked almost too frail to support the harsh northern climate.

With a bow to the guest of honor, she said, "This wine is of poor quality, but it is the best that we have in this backward region. Therefore please accept it as a mark of our respect."

She spoke with a marked Western accent that sounded soft and musical compared to the staccato speech of the northern warriors. Acknowledging the envoy's thanks, she retreated outside the square of diners and sat down to direct her women in serving the wine.

Matsuzo suspected that curiosity about the guests had prompted her appearance at the party, for she looked at the envoy and his retainer Saemon with keen interest. He even found her thoughtful gaze on himself and Zenta. Without joining the conversation of the diners, she examined in turn each of the visitors to the castle.

Conversation in the room was losing its struggle for survival. The usual coarse jests heard in a drinking party did not flourish in the envoy's hearing, and with Lady Kaede's added presence, even milder attempts at humor died down.

The chamberlain began to look desperate as the stretches of silence grew longer and longer. Made bold by the saké, he finally turned to the envoy and said, "Have you attended many drinking parties at the daimyo's castle together with Lord Okudaira?"

"No," replied the envoy curtly. "I've had very few opportunities to do so."

At this point Zenta looked up from his food at last. With the worst of his hunger pangs satisfied, he seemed ready to make some much needed contribution to the conversation. He addressed the envoy respectfully. "Perhaps you were present on the famous occasion when Lord Okudaira and his friend Lord Mochizuki spent the whole evening capping each other's verses to a beautiful lady? Their poetic feats were the talk of the daimyo's capital for weeks."

The envoy's expression grew freezing. "I hardly think that Lord Okudaira's love affair is the proper topic for discussion in the present company!"

Zenta's chopsticks fell from his fingers with a clatter. He sat completely still for several seconds, and then he roused himself and put his chopsticks on their china holder with exaggerated care.

Matsuzo went hot with shame over the public rebuke received by his friend, and for a moment he was filled with an acute dislike for the arrogant envoy. He looked at Lady Kaede for her reaction, and saw that she sat as motionless as a porcelain doll. Her face showed not a trace of expression.

During the next few minutes Zenta busied himself with his food once more. Suddenly he raised his head and addressed the envoy again, evidently willing to risk another rebuke. "Were you at the archery contest in the daimyo's capital last May? All of the daimyo's chief supporters must have taken part. What a glorious pageant it was! It was a pity that the weather was so wet. The muddy ground caused many horses to slip, and several fine archers lost through no fault of theirs."

The envoy seemed to regret his harshness toward the ronin, and this time he answered more pleasantly. "I had to miss that contest, unfortunately. The wet weather started a recurrence of an old illness of mine." He looked at Zenta in some surprise. "Were you there during the contest?"

"I was there in the capacity of an attendant," replied Zenta. "Some of the contestants wanted a little coaching."

There was a bustling in the dining hall. Lady

Kaede had stood up, and she was directing her women to gather up the saké utensils. Cutting short the chamberlain's effusive thanks, she gave a grave nod to the company. Then she arranged her trailing skirt behind her and swept from the room.

With Lady Kaede's departure, the envoy apparently felt that the dinner party had no further claim on his patience. In spite of the chamberlain's eager offer to call in dancers and musicians, he could not be persuaded to stay any longer.

"I know what we shall do," said the chamberlain. "We can take a stroll in the garden to dispel the wine fumes. It would be nice to do some moon viewing, and the more talented of us can make verses."

When the envoy showed no interest in verse making, the chamberlain said hurriedly, "Our garden is noted for its miniature mountain, a most curiously shaped piece of rockery. We should be honored to have your opinion on it."

While the chamberlain gave orders for lanterns to be brought, the dinner guests struggled to their feet. There were some audible groans and some crackling knees. The diners left the room as quickly as good manners permitted, glad to escape the discomfort of the dinner party and find release in the garden.

Chapter 7

"We need more light here," grumbled the chamberlain. "I just bumped my toe against this rock!"

In a few minutes lanterns were bobbing here and there, held by the serving girls to help the guests along the treacherously twisting paths. In the flickering light the garden had the fantastical look of a scene from an old fairy tale.

"Now, who is going to be the first person with a poem to the autumn moon?" asked the chamberlain.

Zenta noticed that Matsuzo was the only person to respond enthusiastically. His young friend would certainly not miss this opportunity to indulge in his favorite pastime.

The idea of a moon-viewing party originated with the noblemen of the imperial court at Miyako, who were experts at elaborate diversions. At first the members of the warrior class had been contemptuous of the nobles and their decadent life. But gradually many of the more wealthy warlords began to adopt the practices of the noblemen.

Zenta suspected that the moon-viewing mound in Lord Okudaira's castle had been built at the suggestion of Lady Kaede. A noblewoman herself, she was familiar with the life of the imperial court.

Zenta smiled to himself as he watched the castle samurai blunder about the twisted paths of the garden, dutifully uttering praises to the moon. As practiced by these provincial warriors, the moon-viewing party became a grotesque exercise.

Curious to see what the envoy made of all this, he looked around until he caught sight of that official. The other man was, in fact, looking in his direction, and he suddenly had the conviction that the envoy was simply waiting for an opportunity to speak privately with him.

As soon as the envoy caught Zenta's eye, he began slowly approaching. The chamberlain, talking without pause, followed his guest of honor. The other man's coldness only increased his efforts to please, and the envoy soon had the frustrated expression of a man who could not shake off a buzzing fly.

"Ah, these gifted young people!" exclaimed the chamberlain, pointing to Matsuzo who was already reciting his first verses to the moon. "How it brings back memories of my own youth when I used to compose poetry right in the face of danger!"

The envoy's interest in the chamberlain's youth did not seem to have increased since dinner. He merely gave a curt nod and moved off, trying to edge his way around the chamberlain's portly figure toward Zenta.

"Please don't overlook this beautiful stone

lantern!" said the chamberlain, following his guest closely. "I'm told that it is older than the castle itself."

Help for the envoy arrived in the form of his chief retainer, Saemon. "I know that you are an expert on poetry, sir," he said to the chamberlain. "Can you come and settle our dispute? One of the men claimed that by giving the Chinese reading to the word, he would have the proper number of syllables in his poem. The rest of us said that this should not be allowed."

Zenta frankly doubted that there was such a poetic dispute. Most of the samurai he saw didn't look capable of writing any poetry at all, much less worry about the Chinese reading of a word.

The chamberlain, however, looked greatly flattered by Saemon's request and allowed himself to be led away. While he was arbitrating in the dispute, the envoy beckoned to Zenta, and the two men walked away until they were at the edge of an artificial pond.

But the chamberlain dealt with the poetic dispute all too quickly. Looking around frantically, he found his guest of honor. "Ah, yes, I see that you are admiring that rock," he cried, panting a little as he ran up to the two men. "This is the volcanic rock that I was telling you about. What a matchless shape! After contemplating it, I always feel that my spirit has been refreshed!"

Saemon suddenly appeared out of the shadows. Just as he reached the group by the pond, he stumbled and fell heavily against the chamberlain.

Zenta heard a cry, followed by a loud splash.

"I'm so sorry!" cried Saemon. "How clumsy of me!"

"You tripped me!" yelled the chamberlain, splashing and floundering in the water.

Zenta and Saemon both leaned over the pond and offered their hands. But the bank was muddy, and the chamberlain slipped back several times before they finally succeeded in pulling him out of the water.

"I certainly hope that the dye of your gorgeous kimono is colorfast," said Saemon as he tried to wring water from his victim's dripping sleeves.

The chamberlain snatched his sleeves from Saemon's hands and glared with red eyes at the envoy's chief retainer. Then he turned away and stalked off furiously.

When his squelching footsteps receded, Saemon grinned at his master, bowed, and tactfully moved away.

For the moment, the envoy had the privacy that he desired. But it was not likely to last long, and he did not waste time in coming to the point. "You announced this afternoon that you intended to serve the new lord of the castle," he said to the ronin. "Are you still of the same mind?"

"I still plan to serve the designated successor

to Lord Okudaira," replied Zenta. "Would it be too presumptuous to ask what the daimyo's exact instructions are on the succession?"

The question seemed to displease the envoy. "The daimyo is some distance away, and he is leaving the local situation to me," he said coldly. "He would like to respect the wishes of his late friend Lord Okudaira, but he thinks it more important to have a seasoned warrior here as commander."

Since Ume had said almost exactly the same thing, Zenta began to have a strong suspicion that the envoy and Lady Tama's people were working closely together.

"It is possible that you could influence the choice of successor here," continued the envoy. "As you know, this castle is well fortified against attack. Therefore my master is likely to accept anyone who is actually in command here, provided that he has a legitimate claim to the succession."

Again, these were almost Ume's words. Did the envoy hear them from Lady Tama, or did she hear them from him? Hiding a smile, Zenta said, "The chamberlain is in command here, and he can make his claim legitimate by marrying Lady Tama."

"Lady Tama will never marry that upstart!" exclaimed the envoy. "He is only a distant relative, and she despises him!"

The envoy spoke so vehemently that Zenta wondered if he was in love with Lady Tama.

He cleared his throat and said cautiously, "Speaking of legitimate claims, what about Lord Yoshiteru? Didn't his father name him as successor?"

"Yoshiteru is too young, and this castle is too strategic for the daimyo to take a risk on the succession," said the envoy impatiently.

Still more familiar words, thought Zenta and waited.

Nor did the envoy disappoint him. "We should consider Shigeteru, the older son. The daimyo would be more than happy to confirm his title once he is installed here as commander."

"And what is my role in this plan?" asked Zenta.

The envoy ignored the irony in Zenta's voice. "This afternoon in the courtyard, you not only disrupted the morale of the castle, but you also succeeded in gaining the respect of the samurai here. Having a swordsman like you in the right place at the right time can be a decisive factor."

Zenta was silent. When Ume had suggested the same thing that afternoon, he had dismissed it as an impossible dream. But that was before he knew that the envoy was in alliance with Lady Tama's forces. He had to feel his way very carefully if he didn't wish to antagonize this powerful alliance.

The envoy said, "You must have come to the castle with the intention of acting in the succession dispute here. We are offering you an opportunity that any ambitious man would pray for. But if you persist on going your own way and acting independently, you may find the climate here very unhealthy."

At this unmistakable threat, Zenta laughed softly. "Are you referring to pests in the bath-house, by any chance? I thought that was the work of a servant girl with a childish sense of humor."

The envoy's smile was grim. "It was a warning, as you know perfectly well. Next time the cold thing on your neck may be a dagger."

"What if I become so frightened by your threats that I run to the chamberlain and report all your plans?"

This time it was the envoy's turn to laugh softly. "We are confident that you will not do that. You see, Saemon knows your reputation. From your past history, he knows that you would refuse to serve a master whom you despise. And how can you help despising that fat chamberlain with his gaudy . . ."

Zenta was holding up a warning hand for silence. He had heard a faint sound, like someone's foot crunching on gravel. When the sound was not repeated, he turned to the envoy and said, "The chamberlain may not have good taste in clothes, but he is quite capable of posting spies all around. You should be more careful of what you say. Otherwise *you* will find the climate here unhealthy also."

"Why should I be frightened of the chamberlain?" said the envoy contemptuously. "He knows that the daimyo would send an army if anything should happen to his envoy."

Zenta was beginning to lose patience with the envoy's arrogance. Trying hard to preserve a respectful tone, he said, "This is a well-fortified castle, as you pointed out yourself. If anything happens to you, the daimyo will not try to attack this castle unless he has absolute proof of the chamberlain's guilt. And the chamberlain will try to suppress the proof. He will have no trouble finding a scapegoat to take the blame."

The envoy was unmoved. "Saemon will see to my safety. Before he kills me, the chamberlain will have to kill every one of my men, and that is not something which he will find easy to hide."

"I suggest that you double your precautions to guard yourself, then. How many men do you have?"

"We have forty men, not counting baggage carriers."

Zenta made no effort to hide his disapproval. "Forty men? That's not enough for your mission."

"Time was short!" said the envoy impatiently. "I was not collecting an army in order to lay siege to the castle! Would it reassure you to know that these men were personally selected by Saemon himself?"

Once again Zenta heard a faint sound, and

this time he knew that it was not his imagination. "Perhaps we should postpone our discussion, since it's getting quite late," he murmured as he saw a dark figure appear behind the envoy.

Jihei had arrived with his noiseless tread. "My master sent me to see that our guests are not being neglected," he announced. "Please tell me how I can be of service."

The envoy looked at him coldly. "It is time for me to retire. I have no need for your services any further tonight."

Then he leaned over and whispered to Zenta, "We must continue our discussion. Come to my room tonight when it is quiet."

Jihei looked at the departing envoy, and his expression was sardonic. "I think that the party is coming to an end," he told Zenta. "It's time to settle down for a good rest."

"Oh, I agree entirely," said Zenta. "I'm ready for bed myself."

He wondered how much of the conversation between himself and the envoy Jihei had overheard. On the whole, he thought pessimistically, he had better assume that Jihei had heard too much.

Chapter 8

Zenta had his own ideas about how to spend the quiet night ahead. As soon as Jihei was out of sight, he looked around for Matsuzo. He needed an agile companion for his coming plans this night, and his young friend was the only person in the castle that he could trust.

But Matsuzo was not to be seen. He was probably off somewhere to admire the moon and compose poetry. Zenta felt rather sorry for the young ronin. He knew that Matsuzo had come from a well-bred family and was used to comfort, and yet he had never questioned Zenta about his plans or complained about the hardships. Smiling faintly, Zenta decided to let Matsuzo enjoy his poetry in peace for the time being. He looked around to make sure that no one was watching, and then he made for the direction of the women's quarters.

Walking very softly himself, he heard the sound of approaching footsteps at once. He quickly stepped behind some bushes. Peeking out between the branches, he saw two figures creeping stealthily down the path: a woman holding a paper lantern, and a small boy clutching a bamboo cricket cage.

"Hold the lantern lower so they won't see our light," whispered the boy, who looked about nine years old. He showed the guilty glee of a child out late at night without his mother's permission.

"Yes, but please keep your voice down," warned the woman. She was dressed in some light-colored garment that floated a little in the evening breeze.

"Why are we going so far?" asked the boy. "I thought that the best crickets are near the foot of the stone walls."

The soft voice of the woman was sweetly persuasive. "You told me that you wanted the biggest and noisiest cricket we could find, didn't you? Well, I happen to know that the best ones are in the cracks between the stones of the bridge over the moat. Won't everybody be impressed tomorrow when you show them what you've got in your cage!"

Noiselessly, Zenta left his hiding place and began to follow the woman and the boy, keeping a distance of about ten paces. As the silent procession moved along, he began to wonder why they had not run into any guards. Considering the chamberlain's nervousness about an attempted insurrection, one would expect to find armed men posted about. Was it possible that the chamberlain had given orders for his men not to interfere with what the woman was doing?

She led the boy through a small gate. By the time Zenta had passed through in his turn, the boy was standing at the very edge of the moat with the woman right behind him. Slowly, she raised her hand. Her intention was unmistakable.

Zenta lost no time. He covered the distance to the woman in four swift strides. Grasping her by the collar, he asked, "What are you doing?"

The woman choked back the beginnings of a shriek and dropped her lantern.

With a swoop, Zenta caught it before it fell to the ground. It was still lighted. He held it up to examine her, but she hid her face behind her sleeve.

Then he turned to the little boy, who stood trembling so hard that the cricket cage rattled in his hand. "Isn't it time for you to go to bed?" Zenta asked.

The boy looked to the woman for support. Finding none, he controlled his trembling, drew himself up and held his head high. "I am Okudaira Yoshiteru, and this is my father's castle." Then some of his dignity faded, and in a slightly defensive tone he added, "I don't see why you should care about my bedtime. Who are you, anyway?"

So this was Yoshiteru. With his sturdy build and his determined stance, the boy was a small version of Lord Okudaira.

Zenta found himself smiling. "My name is Konishi Zenta. I was taking a walk to clear some wine fumes from my head, and I saw your light. Earlier I noticed that the banks of the moat were slippery in some places. When I saw you standing at the edge, I was afraid that you were an intoxicated guest about to fall into the water. Please excuse my intrusion."

The boy nodded graciously to acknowledge the apology. Then his mouth dropped open. "Konishi Zenta! You must be the warrior who arrived this afternoon and turned all the chamberlain's men upside down! I wish I had seen that fight!"

"You didn't miss anything interesting, only some rather clumsy tumbling about," said Zenta. Then he put his hand out. "May I look at your cricket cage? What an elegant one! I used to collect crickets when I was a boy, and some of mine were champions."

As the boy proudly showed off his cricket cage, Zenta asked casually, "Do you often go out at night to hunt crickets? How does your mother feel about your going out so late?"

The boy Yoshiteru looked a little shame-faced. "To tell the truth, my mother doesn't let me go out at all after dark. She is becoming terribly nervous lately. That's why we decided not to tell her about our plan to go out tonight. . . ." He broke off when he found that his woman companion had disappeared. "That's funny, where did she go?"

"What is her name?" asked Zenta. He had seen the woman slipping away, but had decided not to stop her by violent means for fear of alarming Yoshiteru. "Has she been serving your mother for long?"

"No, she's quite new," replied Yoshiteru. "I'm

afraid I don't know her name. You see, after my father died, the chamberlain started to replace our attendants. We have so many new people that I haven't sorted everyone out yet."

"Who thought of going out tonight to hunt crickets?" asked Zenta. "Was it your idea?"

"She suggested it, because she knew how much I liked to collect crickets," replied Yoshiteru. He added defensively, "I can't stay cooped up by a lot of jumpy women all the time, if I want to grow up to be a proper warrior."

"I'm not sure that tonight's expedition was a good idea," said Zenta firmly. "When your mother finds you gone, she will be terribly worried. A proper samurai would not cause unnecessary anxiety to his mother."

"Do you really think so?" asked Yoshiteru. "I suppose you're right, since you are such a great warrior yourself. We'd better go back before my mother starts looking for me, then."

As they started back, he began to look a little worried. "I'm afraid I don't know how I am going to sneak back into my room again."

"A samurai would not sneak into his room," said Zenta. Seeing that the boy was really looking worried, he added, "Let's go back together. You can leave the explanations to me."

"Oh, yes, my mother would listen to *you*," said Yoshiteru eagerly. "I still wish I had seen that fight of yours, though. Can you arrange another fight soon? And make sure that I'm there to see it?"

"I'll do my best," said Zenta gravely. "Is there anyone in particular whom you want me to fight?"

Yoshiteru gave this question serious consideration. "Well, I'd like it to be one of the chamberlain's men again. How about Jihei? I don't care for the way he looks at me sometimes. And he is such a strong man that everybody was afraid of him, until you came along."

"But he kept aloof from the fight this afternoon," said Zenta.

"That was because he thought his men could finish you off without him. Wasn't he surprised!"

As he talked, Yoshiteru led Zenta to the complex of wooden buildings that formed Lady Kaede's apartments. They still had not encountered any guards.

When they were within sight of the buildings, they could hear shrill and excited voices. Yoshiteru's steps began to lag, and he finally stopped altogether. Looking for reassurance from his companion, he said rather dubiously, "You know, you don't look very fierce. How do you frighten your enemies when you fight?"

"Oh, I can look very fierce when I'm fighting. I roll my eyes and cross them like this. Then I gnash my teeth together," said Zenta, and proceeded to demonstrate. Looming over the delighted boy, he gave a terrifying snarl.

Instantly they were surrounded by a group of hysterically excited women. Cries and shrieks came from every side.

"Help! Help!"

"He's threatening our little lord!"

"Save Lord Yoshiteru!"

Some of the women tried to carry off the indignantly kicking boy, while others clutched at Zenta, whose protests were completely drowned out.

From the corner of his eye the ronin caught a flash. He flung himself to one side and barely escaped the swishing blade of a murderous looking weapon.

This was a halberd, a broad curved knife mounted on a long pole. It was the traditional weapon of women in samurai households. When wielded by a trained fighter, it produced terror in the hearts of strong men.

Zenta was frankly terrified. There were three women wielding halberds, and his attempts to dodge their swings were greatly hampered by lack of space and by the clutching hands of the other women. He did not draw his sword, not wishing to cause unnecessary bloodshed, and he tried to use one of the women as a shield. The ferocious women fighters, however, were willing to cut down one of their own people in order to reach him. He was hampered also by a fatal urge to laugh, which had a weakening effect worse than that of wine or fatigue.

Help finally arrived from an unexpected quarter. Yoshiteru succeeded in escaping from his would-be rescuers. Wiggling through the legs of the women, he came up to the female warriors and grabbed at the handle of a halberd before it could descend again.

"Stop! Stop, you stupid women! Can't you understand? He's my friend! He was just taking me home!"

His high voice finally penetrated the din. One by one, the women fell back. To Zenta's relief, the female warriors stepped back and rested their weapons.

Yoshiteru glared around him. "You were attacking Konishi Zenta, you stupid fools! I was out hunting crickets tonight and I met him by the moat. Since it was late and dark, he kept me company on the way home. You'd better say you're sorry! He can cut off all your heads with just two strokes of his sword if he wanted to."

The circle of women stared in dismay. Then slowly, one by one, they bowed down until their heads were almost touching the ground. They were heard to mumble some unintelligible apologies.

Yoshiteru dismissed them with a lordly gesture and turned to examine Zenta. "Are you hurt?" he asked.

Zenta straightened his torn clothing and grinned ruefully down at the boy. "Well, you've had your desire. You saw me in a fight. If you hadn't come to my rescue, I would have been chopped to pieces by those female Deva Kings."

Yoshiteru grinned. "Those women are pretty frightening, aren't they? My father made them train with the halberd. He heard of a castle which was taken by the enemy, and when all the samurai defenders were killed, it was the women fighters who managed to hold off the besiegers so that the lord had time to commit hara-kiri and escape capture."

"I'm glad to see that you and your mother have such effective protectors," said Zenta.

Yoshiteru's face fell. "We used to have many more of these fighting women, but the chamberlain has been sending them away one by one. Those three are the only ones left." Then he brightened. "But you should see my sister Tama! She is the best halberd fighter of all, and she is equal to ten men!"

"With such high standards as these, any fight that *I* can arrange is sure to be disappointing," murmured Zenta.

One of the women approached and bowed. With her voice now low and humble she addressed Zenta. "My Lady Kaede says that she would like to see you in her reception room so that she can thank you personally for bringing back Lord Yoshiteru. Would you come this way, please."

Zenta gloomily inspected some tears which had already appeared in his new kimono. His clothes had a habit of going to pieces on him. He followed the attendant in with a resigned shrug, hoping that Lady Kaede would not be influenced by appearances.

In the reception room a beautifully painted door slid apart to reveal Lady Kaede seated on

78

a flat silk cushion upon a low dais. Behind her were a hanging scroll painted in the Chinese manner and a flower arrangement. Both, like Lady Kaede's kimono, were striking in their simplicity.

Zenta advanced until there was a distance of three *tatami* mats between him and the dais. Placing his long sword behind him, he made a profound bow. When he raised his head, he found Lady Kaede's eyes resting thoughtfully on him. They were luminous with unshed tears.

In the dining hall which had been brightly lit by tall candles, Lady Kaede's beauty had possessed an inhuman brilliance. Seen closer up, her beauty was just as perfect, but it was softened by the mellow light from a flame burning in a dish of oil.

"I am truly grateful to you for bringing home this disobedient boy," she said in her soft Western accent. "Ever since his absence was discovered, our household has been distracted by anxiety. Thank you for relieving our minds, and for bringing him back to us safe and sound." Her voice faltered a little at the end.

Then she recovered herself and turned to her son, looking at once indulgent and exasperated. "Why haven't you been put to bed?"

"You haven't served any refreshments to our guest yet," Yoshiteru pointed out. "I think he looks hungry."

He turned and asked Zenta, "You would like some tea and confection, wouldn't you? If you go to bed with an empty stomach, you won't be able to sleep well."

Zenta kept a straight face. "Some refreshments would be delightful, but I don't want to put this household to any trouble."

Lady Kaede bit her lips to suppress a smile. She beckoned to an attendant and whispered some instructions.

"Be sure to bring the yellow citron-flavored *yokan*, because I don't like the dark kind," said Yoshiteru. Then he added, "That is, I'm sure our guest prefers the citron-flavored one, too."

After the attendant left, Lady Kaede's smile faded. She turned a careworn face to Zenta and asked, "Was Yoshiteru alone when you found him? How did he get out of the gate?"

"There was a woman with him, but she slipped away after I came," Zenta replied. "I'm afraid I didn't get a good look at her face. Perhaps your son knows who she is." As he spoke, Zenta scanned the female attendants in the room.

Yoshiteru looked sulky. "We've had so many new attendants lately that I can't tell them apart. All I know is that she isn't anyone we've had for very long."

The attendant came back with a lacquered tray and Lady Kaede herself prepared the tea. As Zenta watched her pour hot water into a small bowl and whip the powdered tea, it seemed to him that her tiny hands with their tapering fingers were like the lacy leaves of a miniature maple tree. That was the meaning of her name, after all.

After the attendant had passed the sweet confection to the guest, Lady Kaede permitted her son to take a piece also. Then she summoned a woman to take the boy to bed.

"Let me wait until our guest has finished eating," begged Yoshiteru.

"Go to bed immediately," commanded his mother in an unexpectedly firm voice. "You've caused us enough worry tonight, and I won't have any peace until I know that you are safely in bed."

As he was being dragged out, the boy cast a look at Zenta which seemed to say, "We men have to humor these jittery women, don't we?"

When the door closed behind the boy, Lady Kaede turned to her guest and smiled. "His bedtime has been quite irregular lately, but fortunately he is so healthy that he doesn't seem to miss his rest."

Then her face became grave and she shivered slightly. "I think you have guessed a fact that I've tried to hide from Yoshiteru: Since my husband's death, my son's life has been in constant danger. This woman who took him out tonight must have been sent to murder him!"

Looking at Lady Kaede's frail form, Zenta could hardly bring himself to burden her with the truth. But for Yoshiteru's sake, it was essential that she should know the danger. "Yes, you are right," he said. "That woman was on the point of pushing him into the moat. From now on, your son must never go out with anyone except those whom you trust absolutely."

Lady Kaede did not break down into hysteria. Her slender hands clenched convulsively as she fought for control. "Thank you for telling me," she said huskily.

Zenta realized that under Lady Kaede's fragile exterior, she had strength and determination. Even before coming to the castle, he had already decided to champion Yoshiteru's cause. Now that he had met Lady Kaede and the boy, he was emotionally committed as well. This indomitable woman and her courageous son were worth dying for.

"At this time of danger, wouldn't it be wise for members of Lord Okudaira's family to support each other?" he asked. "Your best plan may be to form an alliance with Lady Tama against the chamberlain."

"Tama has shown me nothing but hostility," said the young widow sadly. "When her father married me, Tama's older brother, whom she idolized, had just been sent away. The double shock of losing her beloved brother and having a stranger become mistress here was too much for her. She became extremely jealous."

"That's merely a childish jealousy which she must have outgrown by now," said Zenta.

"Her jealousy has only deepened as she grew older. It is even extending to Yoshiteru as well. My son is menaced from all directions."

"Surely Lady Tama would not harm Yoshi-teru!" said Zenta. "She must have some feeling for her own brother!"

Lady Kaede sighed. "Yoshiteru is only a half brother. The brother that matters to Tama is Shigeteru. She will do anything to have him instated here."

"Lady Kaede, you are forgetting something important: Shigeteru was disinherited by his father. Your son was regarded as the only rightful heir. I'm sure that the daimyo would respect the wishes of the late Lord Okudaira."

"The daimyo!" cried Lady Kaede. "He is far away, and by the time he gives his decision on the succession, my son may be dead! Furthermore, there is talk that Yoshiteru is too young, and that the daimyo wants a tested warrior as commander."

Zenta had to admit that Lady Kaede was right. This talk of Yoshiteru being too young was not just in her imagination. "At least let me speak for you to Lady Tama," he begged. "You do have one point of agreement, namely neither of you wants her marriage with the chamberlain to take place. I'm sure that you can form some plan to help each other against the enemy."

Lady Kaede's smile was tinged with bitter-ness. "Tama is very beautiful and extremely persuasive. After speaking to her, you will soon find reason for setting Yoshiteru aside." She lifted a sleeve and wiped some tears from her eyes. The perfume that came from her clothes was subtle but intoxicating.

Zenta was enchanted. He wondered whether it was a trick of the light or whether Lady Kaede's lovely eyes really had flecks of gold in them. With a great effort he pulled himself together. While Lady Kaede was accusing Lady Tama of using her beauty to win support, she herself was in the process of bewitching him. After all, the jealousy that she had spoken of could be on both sides. Lady Kaede might also be very jealous of her stepdaughter. He had to reserve his opinion until he had seen Lady Tama.

"Lady Kaede," he said, "in spite of all the rumors, Shigeteru may not be coming to claim the succession at all. Until you have proof, it is too soon to accuse Lady Tama of plotting to supplant your son."

Lady Kaede's lips twisted. "Don't bother with your pretenses. My guess is that you have already spoken with Shigeteru, and you know exactly what his plans are."

Without giving him a chance to reply, she stood up, and with a gentle swish of silk, she was gone.

Chapter 9

At first Matsuzo was too happy mingling once more with a cultured society to be bothered by Zenta's continued absence. When he burst out with poetry on his travels, the common people that he met would stare blankly, or worse, snicker. Now at last he was in the company of people who understood the finer things of life. Or so he thought at first.

It gradually dawned on Matsuzo that the chamberlain's men were actually hard-bitten warriors with no interest at all in the poetic possibilities of the Sixteenth Day Moon. The moon-viewing party was just a pretense to impress the envoy and his men.

Matsuzo realized eventually that his listeners were more interested in his background than in his poetry. They persistently questioned him about his family and his travels, but most of all they wanted to know everything he could tell them about Zenta. Where had he met the ronin? Under what circumstances? How long ago?

Matsuzo soon lost his patience. Pleading fatigue, he rose abruptly and declared himself ready for bed. He felt an urgent need to find Zenta and warn him that the suspicions of the chamberlain's men were by no means over. Their questioning showed that clearly.

But finding Zenta proved to be a problem in that confusing garden of twisted paths. Rounding a bend, Matsuzo came upon two of the envoy's retainers, who were sitting rather morosely on a stone bench. They didn't seem to be enjoying the party very much.

One of them looked up at Matsuzo and said wryly, "Gay, isn't it? From the day we arrived at the castle, there has been a dinner party every night to stretch out the evening. I'm beginning to think that the chamberlain will do anything to put off going to bed. He probably gets nightmares."

Now *these* were truly men of culture, not like those provincial warriors of the castle, thought Matsuzo. Aloud, he said, "You must find the parties here very dull compared to the sophisticated ones given by the daimyo at his capital."

"We don't know anything about the daimyo's parties," said the retainer. "Both of us were ronin when Saemon hired us for the envoy's special mission to this castle. We've never even seen the daimyo."

"Then you are not the envoy's permanent retainers?" asked Matsuzo, surprised. He thought it really remarkable that the envoy had not brought his most trusted men.

"The envoy is too exalted a person to concern himself with selecting and hiring samurai," said the retainer. "Saemon made all the arrangements for assembling the retinue."

"When Saemon told us that we would be part of the retinue of the daimyo's envoy, we were delighted with our luck," said the other retainer. "Little did we know that we'd find ourselves in this strange castle where people look over their shoulders all the time and mutter about white serpents."

"That's not all," said the first retainer. "Let me tell you what happened yesterday. I was taking a walk with Saemon, and by accident we found ourselves near Lady Tama's quarters. Jihei saw us there and set after us with a dozen of his men. One would think that we had indecent designs on the women! When the envoy heard about the incident, he was naturally furious. Jihei had to apologize, but it doesn't alter the fact that they are keeping us under close watch and treating us almost like prisoners."

"The chamberlain's men are certainly in an unnatural state of excitement," said Matsuzo. "Did you hear about our experience at the gate this afternoon? We came here looking for work, and before we knew it twenty armed men started to attack us!"

"The chamberlain's men will be even more excited before the evening is over," said Saemon, coming over to join the three men. "I hear that Jihei is planning to post his men in the women's quarters tonight so that they can catch the White Serpent Ghost if it tries to make an appearance."

"Jihei is determined to expose the ghost as a fraud," said one of the retainers.

"Then we'll have to join the ghost hunt, won't we?" said Saemon.

Matsuzo frowned. He didn't know what Zenta's exact intentions were, but he was certain that they wouldn't want to be actively helping the chamberlain. "I don't think that Zenta and I will be joining you," he said coldly.

"Ah, but our efforts to chase the ghost will be doomed to failure," said Saemon, grinning. "My men and I will see the ghost in all the wrong places, and we will be chasing in a dozen different directions. It is certain to heighten the fun."

Matsuzo finally understood. "In that case I think we'd like to join you after all," he said, laughing. "But where is Zenta? I haven't seen him since we left the dining hall."

Even as he spoke, voices were heard coming down the path. Zenta appeared, escorted by three women of gigantic stature. They were talking animatedly and seemed to be in high spirits. When they saw Saemon's party they stopped. Bowing politely, the women left.

Matsuzo stared after them with fascinated horror. "You have very strange tastes," he told Zenta. He himself much preferred women of dainty build.

"Don't you like these women warriors?"

said the ronin. "They are magnificent fighters, and they gave me some exciting moments a little while ago."

"Speaking of excitement, did you hear about the ghost hunt?" asked Matsuzo. He described Saemon's plans.

Zenta's eyes brightened. "Excellent! I would have suggested such a plan if you hadn't mentioned it first." He and Saemon then began a discussion of strategic ways to post the men.

Two hours later Matsuzo was wondering what had happened to the promised excitement. He was cold from sitting motionless for so long, and he had a terrible cramp in his legs.

In the courtyard at the heart of the castle, the persons of high rank lived in clusters of rooms with their attendants, and the various apartments were connected by zigzagging wooden walks covered against the weather.

Matsuzo was sitting in the shadowed corner of one wooden walk which connected Lady Kaede's apartments with those of Lady Tama. He could just make out Zenta in another corner. Somewhere out of sight, Saemon's men were keeping watch on the walk that led from Lady Tama's rooms to the apartments of the chamberlain.

So far, it had been absolutely quiet, and Matsuzo found it increasingly difficult to stay vigilant. After all, he had had a very long day. He thought about the thick quilts filled with silk floss that he had seen earlier in his room, and he felt an overwhelming longing for bed.

He knew that he was dreaming. In his dream a dark shape was looming over him, and he could see burning eyes staring down at him. He could not move. All his limbs ached, and he felt cold and sick. Then he realized that he was not asleep at all, and that there really was something between him and the moonlight. There was a hiss of someone sucking his breath.

At this sound Matsuzo came fully awake at last. He looked up and found that the huge dark shape standing over him was Jihei.

Matsuzo stumbled to his feet, moving as quickly as his numbed and aching legs would allow. It was not until he was face to face with the other man that he realized Jihei was not looking at him at all.

Jihei was staring at something behind Matsuzo. There was such an expression of fear and loathing on his face that Matsuzo felt nothing on earth could make him turn his head to find out what it was. Suddenly Jihei sent him spinning aside with a hard push and started forward.

Recovering his feet, Matsuzo saw the thing. At the far end of the wooden walk, a long white thing glided around the corner. He caught only a momentary glimpse, but he got an impression of something faintly glistening, something fleshy, more like a monstrous worm than a snake. A face appeared for an instant, a ghastly inhuman face with blue lips and unbelievably huge, staring eyes. What was particularly revolting was that one eye was higher than the other. Matsuzo heard a soft slithering sound, but that was immediately drowned out by a pounding of feet from all directions.

He wasn't sure of the exact moment when the music began. It was probably there all the time, underneath the shouting. In normal circumstances, the bamboo flute was an expressive instrument perfect for rendering plaintive and melancholy music. Coupled with the appearance of the ghost, the gliding notes of the flute had an unearthly effect that sent Matsuzo shivering.

Scuffling broke out on Zenta's part of the wooden walk. Matsuzo heard some angry voices, and above the din he recognized his friend's voice raised in a belligerent tone which he had never heard before. He immediately forgot all about his post and started to run towards the scene of the disturbance. The sight that greeted his eyes brought him up short.

Zenta, by some means or another, had become disgustingly drunk. Waving a saké jar in one hand, he was complaining bitterly about unmannerly oafs who were jostling him on all sides. His flailing arms blocked the way to Jihei's men, unsuccessfully trying to edge past him on the narrow walk. One samurai, more agile than the rest, was on the point of working his way past the obstruction, but the wine jar suddenly came down with a sharp crack against his cheek bone.

"That' s funny," hiccuped Zenta. "I thought that the saké was all gone."

His face streaming with saké and blood, Zenta's infuriated victim had his sword half-way out before his companions stopped him. Then his anger gave way to caution, and he stood sulkily mopping his face while Zenta peered stupidly at him and made sympathetic noises.

When Matsuzo came up, Zenta brightened and said to him, "You're always well prepared, and you must have paper tissue on you. Quick, I need some."

Another one of the men tried to edge by, but Zenta's hand whipped out and caught him by the arm. "Oh, no, I can't let you go without making amends for cutting your cheek open. Here, let me wipe your face."

The object of his attentions tried to protest, but he was being muffled by the paper tissue. His struggles to escape were quite futile. Zenta might be drunk, but his fingers retained their steely strength.

"I think you're wiping the face of the wrong man," Matsuzo pointed out helpfully. "This man *here* is the one who is bleeding."

"Why didn't you say so?" Zenta asked his victim. He pushed the man away and sent him crashing into one of his comrades who had almost succeeded in making his way past the congestion.

"What do you think you are playing at, you fools?" snarled Jihei, running up furiously. He had temporarily abandoned his chase of the ghost in order to find out why his men were in a thick clot on the wooden walk. "What are you waiting for? The ghost went that way!"

"Oh, look at his face, the poor man," crooned Zenta, who had finally located the man with the cut cheek. "The least I can do is to make him a bandage."

He bent over and clumsily attempted to tear a strip off the already ragged hem of his kimono. As he bent over, his sword swung up and tripped the first of the men that surged forward at Jihei's command. A few of the others fell over the first man. During the ensuing scramble, Zenta finally caught Matsuzo's eye and drew his attention to Jihei, who was already charging down the direction taken by the ghost.

Matsuzo caught the message. He turned, breathed a silent prayer to his childhood wrestling teacher and flung himself at Jihei. The result was not quite what he intended. Before he managed to get any sort of a hold, he found himself flying through the air. As he landed, he had time to reflect bitterly that he should have listened to his teacher during wrestling lessons instead of thinking about poetry. Fortunately his fall was cushioned by a thick pile of Jihei's men who, groggy but game, came forward still trying their best to obey their leader's command.

And now it seemed that Jihei and Zenta were entangled together in some way that was puzzling at first. Eventually it became clear that Jihei had put his foot through a hole in the bottom of Zenta's kimono. His frantic efforts to free himself merely made things worse.

As he worked at enlarging the hole, Zenta remarked, "You know, I really shouldn't drink on an empty stomach. Just look at the state of my kimono! And I'm seeing things, too. If I hadn't known that I was drunk, I would have said that I saw a big white worm crawling over there."

Every head swiveled around. In the frozen silence, his long, thin finger pointed unsteadily in the direction of Lady Kaede's apartments.

"People always say that you should eat while you drink," continued Zenta, ignoring the fact that he was losing his audience. Underneath the sound of the retreating footsteps, ghostly flute music was clearly audible again. "It makes you hear things, too," he shouted after their backs.

He waited until the others were out of sight, and then he turned to the puzzled Matsuzo. "Come on. We have a visit to make." His voice had become clear and sober, and he seemed to know exactly where he was going.

Chapter 10

"Where are we going?" asked Matsuzo.

"To Lady Tama's rooms," replied Zenta. He glanced back and saw that no one was watching them.

"Why did you send Jihei's men to Lady Kaede's apartments?" asked Matsuzo. "If they should find traces of the 'ghost' there, it could be very unpleasant for her."

"They won't find a trace," said Zenta. "That's why I'm sending them there. My three female warrior friends will give the searchers a stimulating reception, and keep them occupied long enough for my purposes."

Zenta found the door that he was looking for. Without announcing himself, he swept it open and stepped into the room, signaling Matsuzo to follow and close the door.

It was Ume's bedroom, and they found the old woman lying as if in peaceful slumber. She did not seem surprised by the arrival of the intruders, but her eyes widened when she saw who they were. "So! You have become the chamberlain's henchmen after all," she said bitterly.

Zenta paid no attention to this greeting, but looked slowly around the room, noting that its sparse furnishings provided no room for concealment at all. The clothes chest could be ruled out as a hiding place for the "ghost" since it would be the first place that Jihei's men would search. Next he considered the shelves. They were standing bare. The quilts that were usually stored in them during the day were now spread out on the floor as beds for the night. Ume was lying on her bed and made no move to get up. Zenta stared down at the old woman and thought about her strange determination to stay put in her bed. She stirred uncomfortably and avoided his eyes.

"You are taking our intrusion very calmly," he remarked. "Shouldn't you be terribly indignant at the outrageous search taking place? It doesn't look natural for you to be lying there so peacefully. You should jump up and clutch my arm and scream at me."

In contrast to the calmness in Lady Tama's apartments, screams and yells were coming from the direction of Lady Kaede's apartments. Zenta could hear the sound of doors and shelves being slammed open and shut. That was followed by the sound of resounding slaps, and the screams this time were by no means all female. He could tell that some of them were from the throats of Jihei's men.

Suddenly a girl burst into the room and leaned against the door. She was too overcome to speak, and when she lifted her head, Zenta saw that she was shaking with laughter. It took him a moment to recognize the little maid who had conducted them to the bath that afternoon. With the makeup washed from her face, she looked very much younger.

Finally she recovered her breath. "The searchers are all down at Lady Kaede's apartments. You should have seen Jihei's men trying to get past those women warriors that Lady Kaede has. One of them is almost as tall as Jihei, and when she stood breathing fire into his face, he had to back down . . ." She broke down into giggles and was unable to continue. Then, as she caught sight of the two men, the laughter drained from her face and she turned pale.

Zenta gave her a reassuring smile. "I was responsible for sending Jihei's men to Lady Kaede's rooms. I knew that they would get a much livelier reception down there than here."

The two women said nothing. They glanced at each other, and then stared back uneasily at him. The little maid showed uncertainty. Ume showed outright mistrust.

Zenta was undiscouraged by their expressions. "While the chamberlain's ghost hunters are happily occupied, I should like to take the opportunity to speak to your mistress Lady Tama." After a second he added, "If she isn't too busy to see me."

Ume bared her dreadful teeth and laughed scornfully. "That's outrageous! Why should my lady see a beggarly ruffian like you?" She took in his untidy appearance. The silk kimono which had been new only that afternoon was already torn.

"I have come here to help your mistress," explained Zenta. "But even if I were an enemy, how can you stop me from forcing my way in? The chamberlain's men are already close and they intend to search every room tonight. I merely wish to speak to Lady Tama privately before the rest of them arrive."

The little maid looked ready to be convinced. She had regained her flirtatious expression and started to speak. But Ume stopped her. The old woman was implacable. "Before you enter my mistress's room, you will have to kill me first," she declared.

"We don't have time for heroics," said Zenta impatiently. "Jihei's men may be arriving very soon."

"Show the gentleman in, Ume. I should like to hear what he has to say," said a voice behind the door to the adjoining room.

Zenta started toward the door, but the old woman did not give up her determination to stop him. Still not getting up from her bed, she rolled over, shot out her hand and grasped the bottom of his kimono.

Zenta struggled between laughter and exasperation. "Here, you can keep my hem if you want it so much."

"What are you doing, Ume?" said the voice imperiously. "I said let him come in. At once!"

The door slowly slid open, and Zenta saw a dim figure in the unlighted adjoining room.

"My lady, you mustn't!" cried Ume.

Ignoring her completely, her mistress beckoned to Zenta. With a rip, he freed his kimono from Ume's clutches. He signaled to Matsuzo to watch the outside door, and then turned and followed Lady Tama into the next room.

She did not stop in that room, but crossed over in the dark and pushed open another door. "We will talk in the music room," she said.

The music room was lit by two small lamps standing on the floor. Their light shone on an impressive litter of music books and instruments. Drums of all sizes and shapes stood about like toadstools, and a collection of flutes pointing every which way lay on a small table. Music books, some of them very old and valuable, were scattered all over the room. Clearly Lady Tama's interest and passion for music went far beyond mere ladylike accomplishment.

Zenta looked hard at the collection of flutes. He was sure that one of them was still warm and had droplets of moisture in it.

"Oh, yes, the flute has always been one of my favorite instruments," said Lady Tama sardonically.

He turned and saw her clearly at last. In the light of the lamps, her skin glowed with a pearly sheen as if newly washed. He guessed that Ume had not wanted him to see her mistress before she had a chance to put back her makeup. Lady Tama had removed not only her face powder, but also her lip rouge. With its natural contour revealed, her shapely mouth showed a hint of ruthlessness.

Zenta found himself tongue-tied. He had worked hard to contrive this meeting, but now that he was face to face with her, it was difficult to begin. What he had to say would not be well received by this determined-looking girl.

She seemed amused by his intent scrutiny. "Ume told me that she didn't succeed in recruiting you this afternoon. Does your visit tonight mean that you are joining us after all?"

Zenta cleared his throat. "Lady Tama, Jihei and his men will be here any moment. Shouldn't you paint your face? Otherwise they will suspect that you have just washed it to remove the ghostly makeup."

"They won't venture into my private quarters. If they do, the envoy will hear of it. The chamberlain would not dare to offend the envoy."

Zenta thought of the arrogant envoy. Not only arrogant, but incredibly foolhardy as well. "You cannot place all your hopes on the envoy, Lady Tama. He has been making some careless remarks, and his very life will be in danger if the wrong person were to hear about them."

That shook her. With an abrupt rustle of silk, she got up, opened the door of her bedroom and went to her dressing table, which was behind a folding screen.

Through the open door, Zenta could hear

the clatter of cosmetic jars. He hoped her hands were steady, for a crookedly painted eyebrow or smeared lips would cause speculation.

When she spoke, however, her voice was steady and calm. "Don't just sit there like a fool. Come in and tell me about yourself. Why did you come to this castle?"

Zenta entered and sat facing the screen. "I thought I had made that clear. I was looking for a job."

"Don't evade the question. If you were simply looking for a job, you would have snatched at the chamberlain's offer. He is very generous with my father's money when he's enlisting swordsmen for himself."

Zenta was silent for a moment. Then he said carefully, "I have admired Lord Okudaira for many years, but he died before I could enter his service. Now I should like to serve his successor."

Lady Tama stepped from behind the screen, her makeup completed. The vivid young girl with the scrubbed face was gone, and in her place was a proud aristocratic lady. "Who is my father's successor?" she demanded.

Zenta met her eyes squarely and gave the answer that would anger her. "Your father's successor is Yoshiteru. Who else is there?"

"Yoshiteru is only a child!" cried Lady Tama.

"His mother and his sister will guide him. As for commanding the castle, you can get military advisors."

"You have been talking to Kaede, haven't you?" she said furiously. "These Miyako noble-women are experts at deception. A country warrior like you would stand no chance against them!"

It was a shrewd hit. Zenta admitted he had been dazzled by Lady Kaede's beauty and help-lessness. But that was irrelevant to the situation. "Don't you think that at a crisis like this, Lord Okudaira's family should be united?" he asked.

"If you are speaking of my family, you are forgetting one member," said Lady Tama. "What about my brother Shigeteru?"

Zenta grew alarmed at the way her voice rose. "Lady Tama, be careful of what you're saying."

But she was beyond caution. "Shigeteru is a mature warrior, the kind of commander our daimyo needs for this castle."

Zenta made one more effort. "Lady Tama, when Shigeteru left, you were only about six or seven years old. How do you know what sort of person he would turn out to be? Have you con-sidered the possibility that he is unworthy to succeed his father?"

Lady Tama sprang up in a fury. "Shigeteru is a great warrior! I know, because . . ." She stopped, but it was too late. Her words echoed between them, and she stared at him with con-sternation.

Before Zenta could reply, he heard the sound of heavy feet and banging doors. The search party had arrived.

"Ume will need our help," he said, rising quickly to his feet. He left the room and once more assumed the stumbling walk of a drunkard. Lurching into Ume's room, he saw that it was crowded with men overturning chests and sliding open shelves. Lady Tama followed Zenta into the room, looking bewildered at his sudden transformation.

Jihei's men looked shopworn. After the bruising encounter with the amazons in Lady Kaede's service, they clearly didn't expect opposition of the same caliber here.

"Sorry to intrude. Lady Tama, but we have to search every room of your apartment," said Jihei without ceremony.

"They are looking for a big, fat twenty-foot-long worm that's loose," Zenta explained helpfully to the women. He told Jihei, "I've already looked in the other rooms. There is not a trace."

"I shall see that for myself," said Jihei, and started for the next room.

That finally brought Ume up from her bed. She threw herself in front of the big samurai, but he simply brushed her aside like a piece of lint. Lady Tama stood absolutely still.

Zenta yawned and stretched luxuriously. "I really think that it's my bedtime," he announced, dropping down on Ume's bed. He

pulled up the quilt and made himself comfortable. Jihei's men, ignoring him, started to open
every chest and shelf.

Matsuzo looked down at his friend. Getting
no response, he joined the others and made a
great show of helping with the search. He was
puzzled, however. The white thing that he had
seen was long and substantial. It was not a
wisp of a thing that one of the women could
simply tuck into her sleeve. Nevertheless, from
Zenta's relaxed attitude Matsuzo guessed that
he had already seen furnishings for the ghost,
and furthermore did not expect Jihei's men to
find them. But where could the hiding place
be? The rooms were quite bare.

Evidently Jihei's men were also becoming
discouraged. Most of them poked about rather
listlessly. One man approached Zenta's bed
and prodded the mats around it with the scab-
bard of his sword.

The ronin opened his eyes sleepily and
smiled at him with alcoholic friendliness. "How
did you find things at Lady Kaede's apartment?
Was it more lively there?"

"Lively?" said the man with a shudder. "Listen,
those three female ogres nearly tore us apart.
Do you know what I think? They are not
women at all. They are men in disguise.

Another searcher approached. "You look pretty
comfortable," he told Zenta. "I wish I could . . ."

"Well? Have you finished?" demanded Jihei.
"Did you find any lumps under the mats?" He

had returned to the outer room, and his failure to find any trace of the ghost had not improved his temper.

Zenta looked up at him with a befuddled expression. "Maybe your worm or snake or whatever dissolved and oozed through the cracks in the floor?"

"That's it!" shouted Jihei. "We forgot to look under the floor! Here, take up the tatami!"

The tatami, constructed by stitching a finely woven rush mat over a two-inch thick pad, was in the process of being adopted by the upper classes to cover the floors of their living quarters. When Lady Kaede arrived from Miyako upon her marriage, she had brought a tatami maker with her. Under her direction, the more luxurious rooms of the castle were all covered with these snugly fitting mats.

Jihei's men started to pull up the tatami one by one, standing each one on its side. When the third mat was raised, they uncovered some short boards that lifted up. They had found the hole leading to the crawl space under the floor. Each room had such an emergency exit in case of fire or attack. Half a dozen men followed each other in quick succession down into the hole. They were soon heard scrabbling about in the darkness underneath. The rest of the men left the room to reach the crawl space from the outside. A whole new world had opened up for the happy searchers.

Jihei muttered a curt farewell to the people

in the room and hurried out. Ume and the little maid looked at him stonily. Lady Tama had already retired to the music room, where she sat reading an old music book during the entire search.

When the subterranean searching noises receded into the distance, Zenta got up and straightened his clothes. Walking over and replacing the floor boards and tatami, he said, "Your bed is very comfortable, Ume. The quilting is thick, but light and fluffy. My only complaint is about that big lump on the left side. Were you in a great hurry when you stuffed it?"

Ume's face was all smiles, making her look like a dried persimmon. Her doubts about Zenta had evidently been dispelled by his behavior during the search. "I was the one who had the idea of using the bedding," she said proudly. "As I was airing the silk floss for the quilts one day, I had a sudden inspiration. It doesn't take more than a second or two to stretch this shining stuff into a long thin strip so that it wiggles like a snake. And it is just as easy to stuff it back into the quilts afterwards."

"That was why the long white thing had a glistening, fleshy look," thought Matsuzo. Very clever! The ghastly face with the huge staring eyes was simply skillful makeup. Zenta must have guessed the truth when he saw Ume's reluctance to get up from her bed.

"Why do you think there is so much hatred

between Lady Tama and Lady Kaede?" Zenta asked Ume. "Does your mistress feel the same ill will towards her brother Yoshiteru?"

"Lady Kaede is from one of the noble families of Miyako, not from the warrior class as our lord's family is," said Ume. "My mistress is exceedingly proud, and she hates being considered a provincial by a sophisticated lady from the capital. As for Yoshiteru, he is only Lady Tama's half brother. Naturally my lady has warmer feelings towards the brother who had the same mother."

"Ume, stop chattering and come in here," commanded her mistress from the inner room.

Zenta had one last question. "You were the one who put something down my neck in the bathhouse, weren't you? What was it?"

Ume had the unrepentant glee of a child. "I used cold noodles! I'll never forget how the two of you ran around that courtyard looking for snakes!"

As the two men left Lady Tama's apartments, they could hear the sound of Ume's hoarse laughter all the way down the wooden walk.

Chapter 11

"But it's long after midnight!" protested Matsuzo. "I'm sure the envoy went to bed hours ago. He won't like it at all if we wake him at this time of the night." The two ronin were taking advantage of the disorder caused by the ghost hunt to reach the envoy's quarters unobserved by the chamberlain's men.

"He can't possibly sleep with all this uproar," said Zenta. "Furthermore what I have to tell him is too urgent to wait until morning."

As honored guests of the castle, the envoy and his men occupied a luxurious suite of rooms on the grounds of the inner courtyard, close to the quarters of the chamberlain. His meager retinue was barely adequate to form a guard over the numerous entrances to his rooms.

The two men exchanged greetings with the guards at one of the doors and asked whether Saemon had returned.

"He is still helping to mislead the ghost hunters," said a guard, grinning. "The chamberlain's men are probably giving up by now, and Saemon should be returning shortly. My master left instructions for you not to wait for Saemon but to go into his room immediately."

Pushing aside the sliding door, Zenta stepped

into the principal bedroom of the envoy's apartments. Matsuzo followed him and looked around with wide eyes at the elegance of the furnishings.

In the midst of this luxury, the honored guest of the castle lay stretched out, apparently fast asleep. He was not lying under his bed quilts, which were spread out behind a painted screen. Instead he lay face down on the floor. The upper part of his body rested on what looked like a piece of crimson silk.

Seeing the envoy asleep, Matsuzo shrank back and prepared to leave the room. Zenta did not even hesitate, but continued to approach. Before he reached halfway to the recumbent figure, he suddenly stopped short.

Noticing Zenta's shock, Matsuzo followed his glance and took a closer look at the vivid patch of crimson. In the profound silence of the room, the pounding of his heart felt thunderous.

Zenta drew a shuddering breath. "I am too late," he whispered. "What a fool I was not to foresee this!"

A piercing shriek ripped through the air. Across the room in another doorway stood Lady Tama with Saemon behind her. In her dead white face, her staring eyes were huge and wild. Then her mouth twisted, and she shrieked again and again.

Men started to move in the room behind Zenta and Matsuzo. The guards in the antechamber crowded into the doorway and stared at the tableau in the room.

"You murderer!" cried Lady Tama, her voice cracking. "You pretended to help, but all the time you were really working for the chamberlain!"

Zenta made no reply but merely looked at her with wide unseeing eyes. Nor did he move when she snatched the dagger out of her sash and rushed at him.

It was Matsuzo who moved quickly. He seized her wrist and gave a sharp twist. The dagger fell to the ground by the feet of the dead man. There was an angry growl from Saemon's men.

Fear sharpened Matsuzo's wits. "Lady Tama, listen. We are not the ones who murdered the envoy. Look at our swords. They are clean."

Saemon looked up from his dead master and turned to the guards. "Search them for concealed weapons," he ordered curtly.

The men poured into the room. They stripped Zenta and Matsuzo of their swords and searched the two men for a bloody weapon.

Zenta submitted passively to the rough search, still looking dazed by the murder. Matsuzo was surprised to see his friend so completely stunned. He himself was not deeply moved by the envoy's death, having felt only awe and some dislike for the man. It seemed to him that the chamberlain would eventually receive just punishment for the murder, and the daimyo could simply send another envoy.

Saemon's men finished their search. "We couldn't find any concealed weapon, sir, and there is no sign of a bloodstain on their swords," they reported, obviously disappointed.

Saemon was supporting Lady Tama in his arms. She was nearly choked with weeping. "He's dead!" she sobbed. "We have lost!"

Looking at her, Matsuzo thought, "This is not just regret for losing a promising ally. This looks like the grief of a heartbroken girl."

In the pool of blood, the profile of the dead man was haughty even in death. Matsuzo could not picture the envoy in the role of an ardent lover, but he wouldn't understand the heart of a girl like Lady Tama anyway.

Saemon guided Lady Tama to some cushions and made her sit down. Going over to the body of his master, he carefully pulled apart the bloody kimono to expose the chest. They all saw the wound. It had obviously stopped bleeding some time ago.

Saemon looked up. "Matsuzo was right. Our master was dead long before they arrived. Neither he nor Zenta is the murderer."

"But these men could have killed him and then returned later," said one of the guards weakly. He was unwilling to give up the idea that the culprits were here in their hands.

Saemon examined the wound with a trained eye. "No, I don't think so. He was not killed by a sword. It's clear that a dagger thrust made the

111

wound." His eyes went involuntarily to Lady Tama's dagger which lay on the floor, but it was bright and spotless.

A commotion was heard. The chamberlain and his men pushed themselves unceremoniously into the room. The tall figure of Jihei stood aside to reveal the tubby chamberlain, who looked like an untidy peacock in his hastily donned kimono.

"I rushed over as soon as I heard about the murder," cried the chamberlain.

His eyes fell on Zenta and Matsuzo, still held by the envoy's men. He smiled, and the thoughts that passed through his mind were plain on his face. Things couldn't be better. The unfriendly envoy was dead, and there were two perfect scapegoats to take the blame for the murder. "Very good!" he said happily. "I see that you have already caught the foul murderers. We'll take them and see that they pay for their crime."

"Just a moment," said Saemon, blocking the way as Jihei and his men came forward to take the prisoners. "It's not proven that these two men are the guilty ones."

The chamberlain's air of astonishment was a masterpiece. "But who else is there? Surely you don't think that one of your own men committed the murder?"

"There is another possibility," said Saemon grimly.

"We are wasting time," said Jihei. "These

two men are violent and desperate. We saw that by their behavior in the courtyard this afternoon. For the safety of the castle, they should be immediately locked up."

This brought Zenta's head up. The arrival of the chamberlain and his men seemed to have roused him from his state of shock. "In the murder of the daimyo's own envoy, all suspects should be reserved for questioning by the daimyo himself," he said, looking very deliberately at Jihei. "Anyone tampering with the suspects would come under suspicion."

Jihei reddened furiously, but before he could reply, Saemon said, "That is true. The daimyo would not thank you for administering his justice!"

"That was not my intention!" protested Jihei angrily. "I merely wanted to take these dangerous men into custody. You're not suggesting that we allow them to remain free?"

"What proof do you have that they are dangerous?" demanded Saemon. "So far as we know, their only connection with the crime is that they discovered the body. I know that my master was dead long before they came."

"How could you know what was happening in your master's room?" retorted Jihei. "You and your men were busy distracting us during the ghost hunt. Don't think that we didn't notice."

"The ghost hunt was a perfect cover for many other activities," said Saemon. "I'm not over-

113

looking the fact that your men could have used it as an excuse for breaking into this very room!"

During the heated exchange, Matsuzo noticed that Zenta was staring fixedly at a spot near the envoy's body. When Zenta felt himself observed, he hastily turned his head away. But Matsuzo had already seen what he was staring at. It was the heel half of a bloody footprint. The front half had been obliterated by the spreading pool of blood.

Saemon, whose eyes missed nothing, followed Matsuzo's glance and saw the print also. "Here is something strange!" he exclaimed and pointed. Everyone turned to stare at the print.

Saemon glanced around and examined the feet of every person in the room. None of them were stained with blood. "This print was not made by one of us in the last few minutes. The murderer must have made it after he stabbed my master."

After inspecting the footprint carefully, he continued, "The outline is quite clear, and this means that there was a lot of blood on the foot. The question is, how did the murderer get out of the room without leaving another bloody footprint?"

There was a silence which lasted for some minutes as people entertained visions of the murderer making a giant leap or flying through the air.

"What about the hole that leads to the crawl space under the floor?" asked one of the envoy's men. "Perhaps he escaped through that."

"No, it's too far away," answered Saemon. "When we first arrived, I checked the location of the emergency exit in every room of our suite. The one for this room is in that corner over there. The murderer would have had to jump halfway across the room. You men in the antechamber would have felt the thump as he landed."

Some of the men considered the wooden beams in the ceiling. A very tall man possessing strong arms might be able to jump and grasp one of the beams, but they did not offer a good hold for bare hands, and he would have to let go before proceeding very far.

The most teasing problem was the reason why. Why should the murderer go to the trouble of keeping his feet off the floor?

Suddenly Jihei pointed at Zenta. "This is another one of your tricks," he snarled. "There has been nothing but confusion in this castle from the moment you arrived. I don't know what your plans are, but I fully intend to find out!"

"I was suspicious of him as soon as I saw him this afternoon," said the chamberlain. He ran his tongue over his lips and smiled eagerly. "We have ingenious ways of getting answers to our questions."

"Wait! I can't allow you to do this," cried Saemon. He seemed even more alarmed than the prisoners themselves at the prospect of their being tortured for information.

"This ronin obviously knows more than he is telling," said Jihei roughly. "The daimyo will not object if we present him with a nice confession already signed."

"I believe that's tampering with the suspects," commented Zenta.

"Since it's a question of my master's murder, *my* men and I should have custody of the prisoners," insisted Saemon.

"And since it's a question of the safety of the castle, I propose to take them into custody," retorted Jihei. "I cannot let these criminals have the chance to commit another murder!"

"This is outrageous!" cried Saemon. "Are you implying that the castle is not safe with all forty of us guarding these two unarmed men?"

"We know that these men are exceptionally cunning," said Jihei. "It would be only sensible to let our men keep them safe until the time comes to send them to the daimyo."

"Do you mean that my men are unable to guard them safely," demanded Saemon, "or that we might deliberately allow the suspected murderer of our master to escape?"

Jihei was becoming very angry also. "I am pointing out that our forces are vastly superior to yours. We outnumber you by more than ten to one."

This was clearly a threat, and the envoy's men growled angrily. Saemon ground his teeth, but could not deny the truth of Jihei's statement. The envoy's quarters were in an open wooden structure impossible to defend, and they were surrounded on all sides by the chamberlain's men. Any attempt to resist would end in a bloody massacre. He shook his head warningly at those of his men who were already reaching for their weapons.

Although violence was averted for the moment, the chamberlain was anxious to leave. Looking nervously at the angry faces of Saemon's men, he said to Jihei, "Come on. Let's get the prisoners into the inner fortress."

In his hurry to remove the prisoners and end the tense confrontation with Saemon, the chamberlain made two mistakes. First, he did not take the time to send for rope and have the prisoners bound. Secondly, he failed to pay attention to Lady Tama.

While Saemon and Jihei were engaged in their heated argument, Lady Tama gradually regained her composure. Her face, still swollen with weeping, was set in furious thought. Finally she moved quietly back toward the door and slipped out of the room. None of the chamberlain's men noticed her departure.

Chapter 12

The guards escorting the prisoners to the inter-
rogation chamber surrounded them densely
on all sides as they marched across the inner
courtyard. But when they entered the mazelike
corridors of the inner fortress, they were forced
to string out in a double file. Jihei was far in
front, leading the party. Zenta and Matsuzo
were in the middle of the long file, with some
fifteen men before them and an equal number
behind. No one spoke, and on the polished
wooden floors of the corridor, their sandaled
feet made little noise.

In the forefront Jihei turned a corner which
led in one direction to a long dark hallway and
in another direction to a narrow flight of stairs
going to an upper floor. Suddenly he stopped.
The whole party came to a halt and stood
motionless. Their ears caught the sound of a
flute.

The ghostly flute music became louder, and
in the light of Jihei's lantern they saw a dim
white figure at the end of the hallway. Then it
turned and glided off with a soft slither. A low
laugh echoed down the corridor.

Jihei forgot his prisoners. All he could see
was the hateful figure which had mocked and
humiliated him earlier in the evening. With an

angry hiss he darted forward along the hallway, followed by his eager men.

At the foot of the staircase, Zenta heard a faint noise from above. He looked up and saw Saemon at the top of the stairs with a sword in one hand and a lantern in the other. Saemon did the only thing possible: he threw his sword down to Zenta.

The ronin had been expecting this move from the moment he heard the flute music. He caught the sword neatly. When the guards realized what had happened, they turned and saw the light glinting wickedly on the naked blade as Zenta tested it for balance. "Well, now," he said, his voice purring with pleasure, "I believe you people mentioned something about a lesson in swordsmanship?"

He made a flashing attack on the guards and cleared a space at the foot of the stairs. Before the guards could recover to counterattack, he was already racing up the stairs, pulling Matsuzo with him.

Jihei and the guards in front were halfway down the corridor after the ghost when they heard the sound of the clash behind them. By the time Jihei realized his mistake and struggled back, the prisoners were already at the top of the stairs. Zenta seized the lantern from Saemon and hurled it into the face of the nearest pursuer.

The man flung up his arm to protect his face. His sleeve caught fire and he screamed with terror. Losing his footing, he fell tumbling down the stairs and sent the men behind him toppling.

The castle walls were plastered, but the basic building material was wood. Fire, therefore, never failed to cause unreasoning panic. For some moments complete confusion reigned at the foot of the stairs as the men tried to beat out the flames. Groans came from the men bruised from their fall down the stairs.

The three men at the top of the stairs did not wait to see what was happening. With Zenta leading the way, they ran through the corridors of the upper floor. Down a different flight of stairs they went, through one corridor after another, one turn after another, then up and down some more stairs.

"I hope you know where you are going," Matsuzo managed to gasp with bursting lungs.

Zenta finally stopped. He opened the door of a small guard room, found it empty, and entered it quickly, followed by the other two men. After catching his breath he said, "I think we've lost them for the time being."

"We can't stay here," said Saemon. "Jihei will sound a general alarm soon and search every room. I must gather my men together and find a place where we can defend ourselves."

"I suggest that we try to occupy some tower of the outer fortress," said Zenta. "It is fortified, and much easier to defend than one of the residential buildings. Since most of the samurai there have been ordered to the inner fortress, we can take the place easily."

Suddenly the three men tensed. They heard the sound of running feet. But the men, instead of searching the rooms one by one, rushed past their door. Matsuzo could overhear snatches of conversation.

"Did you see how close the White Serpent was this time? I saw it before I even heard the flute music."

"We'd better hurry. Jihei will have our heads if we fail to catch the ghost again."

Inside the room Matsuzo stared in amazement. "I thought I could run pretty fast," he muttered, "but Lady Tama can run much faster, even trailing a silk floss snake!"

Saemon smiled. "That was not Lady Tama you saw earlier. It was her double. They have two White Serpents, and this is the reason why the ghost hunters were so confused. Each time they started after the ghost, the flute music would come from a totally different direction."

"Then the men that just went by were not pursuing us at all," said Zenta. "They don't even know about our escape."

"That's right," said Saemon. "Lady Tama is distracting the attention of the castle men and scattering them with a ghost hunt, so that Jihei will not be able to round up his men and issue orders."

Matsuzo remembered that earlier Zenta had

said Lady Tama had the mind of a strategist. It was no exaggeration. Zenta now frowned, however. "Lady Tama is courageous, but she's utterly reckless. If she should fall into the hands of the ghost hunters, she would be treated mercilessly. Even worse, the chamberlain may seize the opportunity to violate her, claiming that he didn't recognize her. She would be forced to marry him, then."

"I've already told her this," said Saemon. "But she's very stubborn, and she insisted on playing the White Serpent Ghost one last time. I agree that she is in very great danger. Let me go and rally my men to storm the outer fortress. Meanwhile you and Matsuzo should bring Lady Tama to safety."

There was no time to be lost. After checking that the corridor was clear, Saemon sped off to his waiting men. Zenta led Matsuzo down some stairs, through a series of dark and narrow passages until they came to a small door that opened into the courtyard. This was the clearing between the inner and outer fortresses. Their problem was to find Lady Tama and then cross the moat, and they could expect the bridges to be heavily guarded.

Hearing cries in the distance, they turned and saw a white figure flying toward them. Matsuzo recognized the ghastly face which he had seen earlier, with the same huge staring eyes and blue painted lips. Behind the figure trailed a silk floss tail, somewhat shortened by clutching hands.

The figure almost reached them before Matsuzo recognized Lady Tama. Far from being terrorized by her pursuers, she seemed to be in a state of exhilaration. She had recovered completely from her grief, and Matsuzo had the feeling that her love for the dead envoy had not been very deep.

One of her pursuers reached out a hand and grasped her sleeve. She turned and dealt him a sharp blow across the bridge of his nose with her flute. While the man covered his nose and howled with pain, Lady Tama calmly examined her flute. "What a pity! I made a crack in the flute, and it's my favorite one."

Zenta rushed up and made short work of two other pursuers who had run over to help their comrade.

Lady Tama flashed a fierce grin at her rescuer. "Come on. There are a few more men over there that we can finish. Who knows? Maybe we can take over the castle!"

"Don't be silly," snapped Zenta, sparing no time for courtesies. "We have only one sword among the three of us, and your flute is a limited weapon."

As they ran across the courtyard Lady Tama asked, "What are our plans now? Did Saemon say anything after he freed you from Jihei's men?"

"We have to find shelter, a place that we can temporarily defend," said Zenta. "The best place is . . ."

"The outer fortress, of course," finished Lady Tama.

A cry to their left drew their attention. They saw Ume carrying an armful of weapons, and beside her a figure in white. Matsuzo blinked. He was looking at an exact duplicate of Lady Tama. When the figure came closer, he recognized the little maid. Her makeup and white gown were identical to Lady Tama's.

Zenta, however, had eyes only for the weapons in Ume's arms. "My swords!" he cried joyfully. Snatching his two swords from the old woman, he pulled the long one from its sheath and ran his fingers down the perfect blade. He almost crooned with happiness.

Lady Tama chose one of the halberds that Ume had brought and impatiently pounded its butt on the ground. "A touching reunion! Have you finished fondling your swords? We have some fighting to do before we can cross the bridge over the moat."

Running once again, Zenta asked Ume, "Have you seen Saemon?"

It was the little maid who answered. "Saemon and his men should be attacking the outer fortress by now. I had all the guards at the southern gate on my trail, and Saemon's men slipped through easily."

The progress of the little party was slowed by Ume, who gasped for breath and stumbled with fatigue. "Please forget about me! First get Lady Tama into safety!" she panted.

Zenta and Matsuzo picked her up and between them carried her as they ran. "She looks like a bundle of dry sticks, but she's heavy," thought Matsuzo.

They reached the bridge over the moat and found it guarded by a dozen of the chamberlain's men. Zenta dropped Ume unceremoniously, and with three vicious sweeps of his sword cleared a way for the women.

Instead of crossing the bridge, Lady Tama swung her halberd joyously and joined the battle. Yoshiteru had been right. His sister was a formidable fighter with her halberd. Her ancestors, after all, had risen to their high position through sheer love of fighting.

The engagement did not last long. Zenta alone would have routed their opponents easily. His ferocious female assistant with her ghostly makeup and her whirling halberd reduced them to terror. The chamberlain's men turned and fled.

Lady Tama was in favor of pursuing them, but Zenta pulled her back. "There's no time for that!" he said. "The chamberlain will call out his archers at any moment, and we have to find shelter immediately. You're a perfect target in that white gown."

"They won't dare to shoot at me!" she cried indignantly.

"How can they recognize you in that makeup? They can't tell you and the little maid apart, and they won't hesitate to shoot either of you."

Picking up Ume once more, they hurried on, meeting only scattered parties of castle men whom they easily brushed aside. When they finally reached one of the towers of the outer fortress, they found the battle there almost over.

One of Saemon's men was at the door, and he greeted them triumphantly. "You've managed to get through! Saemon will be delighted to hear this!"

"Did you succeed in occupying the tower?" asked Lady Tama.

The man nodded. "We had very little trouble. There were only a few men stationed here, and we took them completely by surprise."

Recovering his breath, Zenta said, "Since you don't need my help here, I'm going back. I must see that Yoshiteru is safe."

"What?" exclaimed Lady Tama. "After all the trouble we took to get you out? You must be insane!"

"Of course I'm grateful for the rescue," said Zenta. "Now that I'm fully armed, there's no need to worry. With all the confusion caused by the ghost hunt and the escape of Saemon's men, I should be able to reach Yoshiteru."

Matsuzo took Zenta by the arm. "Lady Tama is right. It would be suicide to go back. The whole garrison is out looking for you."

"I know why you are going back!" said Lady Tama furiously. "It's not for Yoshiteru's sake. You're in love with his mother!"

There was a hiss and a thud.

"They've called out the archers. Stop arguing and get in," said Zenta, swinging Lady Tama behind him.

There was another hiss, and Zenta stiffened. He reached up to pluck weakly at the shaft buried in his left shoulder. Then with a faint sigh, he dropped his hand and began to fall.

Arrows came faster. With the help of Lady Tama, Matsuzo dragged Zenta inside the door of the fortress. They were followed quickly by Ume and the little maid. Lady Tama slammed the door shut.

The first thing that Matsuzo saw in the dim light was Saemon's face.

"Please honor our humble home," he said.

Chapter 13

"The chamberlain's men are completely bewildered," said Lady Tama with satisfaction. "Half of them are searching for the escaped prisoners, and the rest are hunting for the White Serpent Ghost. It will be a long time before they realize that Saemon and all of his men have broken out of the inner courtyard."

After arriving safely in the tower, she had scrubbed her face clean. With her hair tied back, she looked like a mischievous page boy of some daimyo. She seemed thoroughly at home in the crowded guardroom full of men and weapons.

"Perhaps the chamberlain will think that Shigeteru has finally arrived and started his insurrection," said Matsuzo, grinning. He was unprepared for the reaction to his joking remark. Saemon stared at him with narrowed eyes, and Lady Tama turned rather pale.

Saemon recovered himself and said briskly, "We must have our defenses ready before the chamberlain discovers what the true situation is. Our position here could be worse. We have a number of good archers among our men, and more arrows than we need. We can defend every entrance to this tower. The castle men will find it very costly if they try to rush either of the bridges across the moat."

So far, several small parties of the chamberlain's men had tried to enter the tower in pursuit of the fugitives, but they had been mercilessly cut down by Saemon's archers. After viewing their losses, the chamberlain's men had decided that it was not worth the trouble of going after the two escaped prisoners. They were still under the impression that the fugitives would be easily subdued by their men in the outer fortress.

But sooner or later they would discover the exodus of the envoy's men and learn that a portion of the outer fortress was in their hands. Saemon was losing no time in marshaling his small army. He quickly scanned the list of names compiled by one of his men. "We have thirty-seven fighting men, two killed and three wounded."

"Count me as one of the fighting men," declared Lady Tama.

Saemon smiled at her. "Very well, thirty-eight fighting men. We can't afford a pitched battle since we are badly outnumbered, but our position here is not hopeless."

He looked down regretfully at Zenta, who was having his shoulder bandaged by Ume. "The chance arrow that hit you was our worst piece of luck so far. We had been counting heavily on having your sword on our side."

"I can still manage a sword with one hand," said Zenta.

"So long as the chamberlain's men don't know that I've been hit, I can be useful by just frightening them a little."

"You need more practice in looking fierce," said Matsuzo, and the others laughed.

Zenta did not share the general cheerfulness. He was in pain from the extraction of the arrow, and he was chafing with frustration at not being able to return to the inner courtyard.

Lady Tama merely laughed at his ill humor. She said, "Something amusing has just struck me: In a sense, we are standing siege here."

There were some chuckles in the room, and one man remarked, "We are the besieged, but we are outside of the besiegers in the inner fortress. This will make military history."

"We're well prepared to stand siege," said Lady Tama. "There are plenty of arrows and spears here, and enough armor to outfit each man."

Matsuzo looked at Zenta and smiled. "I hope we didn't forget to provide ourselves with plenty of food."

Zenta did not return the smile. "Before you see yourselves as the victors of White Serpent Castle, you should remember that we are outnumbered roughly ten to one. Furthermore, our windows facing the inside are all cut wrong for effective shooting. After all, the castle was not constructed for the purpose of helping

130

people in the outer fortress attack those in the center."

Saemon said impatiently, "There is no question of our attacking the chamberlain. We are not cut off. Whenever we wish, we can send men down into the village to collect help."

Something had been puzzling Matsuzo since the discussion had started. If even Lady Tama joined freely in the council of war, why should he be too shy to speak up? "What is to prevent us from leaving the castle?" he asked. "Then you and your men can go back to the daimyo and report the envoy's murder to him."

For a moment, no one spoke. Lady Tama and Saemon exchanged glances.

Saemon seemed to choose his words carefully as he replied, "There is the question of vengeance. My master has been foully murdered, and I cannot leave until I see his murderer punished."

"But without help you have no hope of defeating the chamberlain and arresting the murderer," objected Matsuzo. "You need reinforcement from the daimyo. When he hears of his envoy's death, he will rush a strong force here. While I admire your determination to take action yourself, you would only die in vain."

Again there was an odd little silence.

It was Zenta who finally broke the silence. "No, we can't leave the protection of the fortress here. If we abandon our position and retreat

131

to the village, there is nothing to check the chamberlain's men from cutting us down in the open. We're trapped here for the moment."

Matsuzo was surprised. It was uncharacteristic of his friend to be so pessimistic.

Lady Tama glared at Zenta. "Really, I don't know why we bothered to rescue you at all when you just sit there spreading gloom and despondency. If this goes on, we'll be defeated by your talk alone!"

Zenta struggled to his feet. "Then the best thing is for me to return to the inner fortress and spread gloom and despondency to the chamberlain's men."

Saemon quickly barred his way. "You are not going anywhere. Sit down!" he ordered curtly. Some of his men stirred.

Zenta's eyes flashed and his hand dropped to his sword. For a moment violence seemed about to erupt. Then with an obvious effort he controlled his temper, and when he spoke his voice was level. "What plans have you really made for conducting your little war here? You are temporarily safe because the chamberlain doesn't know the full extent of what has happened. But it won't take him too long to find out. And Jihei is no fool. What if he organizes his men and starts a general attack on you? Your archers won't hold them. I should be surprised if you lasted more than half an hour."

Ignoring the angry and defiant muttering from the men around him, he continued, "Very well. To avenge your master's death you are resolved to die heroically. But have you thought about Lady Tama? What do you think her fate will be?"

"I'm prepared to die with the men," declared Lady Tama.

"But the chamberlain might capture you alive," said Zenta. "He might do anything to you then. Afterwards he could claim he was carried away by the heat of battle. Do you expect the White Serpent to come and rescue you?"

"I will never let them take me alive!" she cried fiercely.

In spite of himself, Zenta had to laugh when he saw her warlike expression. "Now who is being gloomy and despondent?"

"I will never marry the chamberlain," muttered Lady Tama. "Death is preferable!"

"Before you all resign yourselves to a heroic death, listen to my plan at least," urged Zenta. "We can't afford to sit here and allow Jihei time to organize an attack on us. We have to start winning the castle men to our side at once."

"But how?" demanded Lady Tama. "We can't just shout, 'Come and join us!'"

"Of course not," said Zenta. "What I plan to do is approach the men a few at a time and use quiet persuasion. Although the castle men have been hired by the chamberlain, they have officially sworn allegiance to Lord Okudaira. We can appeal to them as samurai to honor this allegiance."

Several people nodded agreement.

"Until he marries Lady Tama, the chamberlain is not the legitimate ruler here," continued Zenta. "I shall tell the men that their first duty is to Lord Okudaira's family. That family now consists of Lady Tama and Yoshiteru, and no other. The men of the castle also have a duty to help the envoy's men, who were forced to flee from the inner fortress because they were afraid for their lives. If we succeed in getting a sizable portion of the men to our side, we may have a chance."

Saemon considered the proposal in silence for some minutes. "Your plan might work," he said finally. "But instead of sending you, I prefer to send some of the chamberlain's men that we have here as prisoners. They will make good spokesmen for us, and their comrades will believe them more readily."

Realizing that there was no hope of persuading Saemon to release him, Zenta said wryly, "All right, let's bring in the prisoners and try to convince them."

Saemon gave a command. After a few minutes a dozen of the castle men were led into the room. They blinked at the company. From their expression it was obvious that they were wondering why the envoy's men, honored guests of the castle, should suddenly rise and overrun the outer fortress.

"Unbind them," ordered Saemon. His men took out their swords and cut the ropes with

134

ropes with quick, efficient flicks. The prisoners rubbed their arms and looked more bewildered than ever.

Saemon drew himself up to his full height. He passed his eyes slowly over the castle men and cleared his throat impressively. "I can see that you are all loyal men of the castle, resolved to do your duty to Lord Okudaira's family. The time has come to test that loyalty."

It was a good beginning. Every samurai has been trained from early childhood to loyalty for his feudal lord and family.

"As you know," continued Saemon, "the cham- berlain has sworn to be a faithful vassal of Lord Okudaira. Let us look at his behavior towards his lord's family. First, in violation of civilized behavior, he ordered his men into the ladies' private quarters. Next, he actually ordered his men to attack Lady Tama! In desperation, the poor lady has fled to us for protection."

Saemon pointed, and the men turned to stare at Lady Tama. They couldn't recognize their lord's proud daughter in that slim boyish figure.

Then Ume laughed hoarsely. "You stupid fools! You can't recognize Lady Tama just because she washed her face and tied her hair back?"

A few of the men smiled. They had no difficulty recognizing Ume at least.

Next Saemon indicated Zenta and Matsuzo.

"As some of you know, these two gentle-men came to the castle with the intention of serving Lord Okudaira's family. Because they refused to enter the chamberlain's service exclusively, he ordered them arrested at once. It was only my master's timely arrival which saved their lives."

Saemon was twisting the truth a little, but his story had a plausible sound, since most of the castle had heard about the fight in the courtyard and the envoy's intervention.

"Not content with that, the chamberlain has tried to place the blame for my master's mur-der on these two innocent newcomers. But my men and I are not deceived by his lies. We believe that the real killer of my master is somewhere in the inner fortress. We fled from there to save ourselves from being massacred.

"I ask you, as true samurai and men of honor, to make your choice. Should you con-tinue to serve this usurping chamberlain, whose ambition will lead him to certain ruin? Or should you cast your lot with us?"

The prisoners whispered among them-selves, and after a while they nodded. One man came forward to act as spokesman for the rest. "We believe that our duty is here with you. Tell us what to do and we will obey."

Lady Tama's face glowed. Saemon per-mitted himself a grave smile as he addressed the men. "I was sure I could count on loyal men like you. The daimyo will hear of this when I report to him. And Lady Tama is rejoicing in your loyalty to her family."

Lady Tama responded to Saemon's cue and gave the men an encouraging smile.

Saemon continued. "You say that you wish to help our cause. I have a task for you that is dangerous, one which only the brave will under- take. I ask you to go to the inner fortress and find as many of your friends as you can so that you can tell them the whole truth. Tell them how Lady Tama came to us for protection from the chamberlain's attacks, and how we fled here to escape the fate of our master. When your friends hear you, they will all join us in overcoming these murderers!"

His listeners looked shaken. It was easy enough to say that they saw the truth, but if they were caught proclaiming it by Jihei, they could expect no mercy. They shuffled uncomfortably and avoided each other's eye.

Saemon had expected this hesitation, and he now brought out his strongest argument which he had saved for this moment, "We have already dispatched a messenger to the daimyo to report on the murder. If this castle is still in the hands of the usurper chamberlain when the daimyo arrives with his army, the daimyo will reduce the castle to rubble and put every-one to the sword."

No messenger had been sent to the daimyo, but the prisoners could not know this. The daimyo was one of the notable warriors of the day, and the thought of his avenging army descending on the castle was as terrifying as Jihei's wrath. Finally the man who had been their spokesman bowed and said that he would obey. The others slowly followed his example.

Saemon gave orders for their weapons to be returned to them. Then they were let out one by one, not all from the same door. A few looked frightened but resolute, while others could not conceal an air of relief.

Looking at the latter, Matsuzo said dubiously, "Some of these men might join the chamberlain's side again as soon as they get back, and some others looked as if they would just go and hide themselves."

"Many of them probably will," answered Saemon. "Let's hope that enough of them will have the courage to carry out their promise. Fortunately for us, our news is the kind that spreads like fire once it starts."

The first indication of their success came less than an hour later.

"The watch for the door facing south reports that a number of men are approaching!" shouted a man rushing into the room.

Saemon ran. When he arrived at the southern gate, the watchman had a second report for him. "They are shouting that they have a message for us. There is a man holding a written message from the chamberlain. He wants us to admit him."

"Tell him to approach alone," ordered Sae-mon. "Tell him that we have arrows trained on all the rest."

As his men leaned out to transmit his orders, Saemon turned triumphantly to Lady Tama. "The men we sent must have done some good after all! I think wc are winning some of the garrison over."

Lady Tama laughed happily. "I think you're right! If the chamberlain is ready to parley, he must be frightened. Otherwise he would simply order a general attack."

"Here is the messenger, sir," announccd one of his men.

The messenger from the chamberlain bowed deeply to Saemon as he presented the paper. The awe that the castle men had felt for the envoy still extended to his chief retainer.

While Sacmon read the letter, the mes-senger examined the company curiously. He stared hard at Lady Tama until he recognized her. Then he blushed in confusion and lowered his eyes.

"The impudent barefaced liar!" exclaimed Saemon. "He says that we have kidnapped you and are holding you here against your will. He orders us to send you back immediately." He gave a furious laugh and handed the letter to Lady Tama.

After reading the paper she turned to the messenger. "Look at me. Do I seem like a helpless prisoner? Go back and tell the chamberlain I loathe him so much that I would rather kill myself than return!"

"Wait, I want to ask this man something before we send him back," said Saemon. "What happened to the men whom we captured here and then released?"

The messenger looked very frightened. "I didn't see any of them myself," he stammered. "But I was told that some of them were spreading lies. They were causing so much alarm that Jihei gave orders for them to be arrested."

There was a stir in the room. This was good news. The fact that Jihei felt it necessary to take action meant that the castle men were seriously disturbed by the developments.

"You can now see for yourself that those men were not telling lies, but the truth," Saemon told the messenger. "Go back to the chamberlain and tell him that Lady Tama is staying here. Soon all loyal samurai of the castle will come to her side."

When the messenger left, Lady Tama said softly, "I think it's going to work! Did you see that messenger's face? We convinced him that as long as I am with you, the chamberlain has no legitimate standing."

"I think that there is enough doubt and unrest, anyway, to prevent Jihei from mustering his men for a general attack on us," said Saemon.

"The longer they wait, the better it is for us," said Lady Tama. "They will have time to worry about the daimyo's anger falling on their heads. Every minute passed increases their fear."

As the little army in the outer fortress waited, their hopes grew that the enemy was really being disrupted by uncertainty and dissension. The castle had been under great tension, and the time was right for an insurrection.

Ume had some beds prepared. Several times she asked her mistress to lie down and try to sleep, but Lady Tama was too excited to rest. Zenta was the only person to make use of the beds. Stretching out and closing his eyes, he cut himself off from the discussion and speculation taking place all around him.

Then came a cry from the watch. "There is a large procession of men coming! They are stopping at the moat, and they are sending another messenger forward."

The messenger this time was a different man. Perhaps the answer brought back by the other man had infuriated the chamberlain, and the unfortunate messenger had been silenced.

Saemon read the message and crushed the paper in his fist. "The chamberlain says that far from being disloyal to Lord Okudaira's family, he is the champion of the rightful heir. To prove that, he is bringing out Yoshiteru. He says that if we are concerned with the safety of the boy, we should surrender immediately."

For a moment Lady Tama was too angry to speak. "Why, he was the one who kept insisting that Yoshiteru was too young to command here! What does he think he is doing?"

Zenta stared out the window at the group standing near the moat, illuminated by the torches. He saw the small figure of the boy. Standing behind him and holding him by the arms was a woman dressed in white. Zenta's heart contracted with fear. It was too distant to make out her features clearly, but he knew without doubt that this was the woman who took the boy cricket hunting and tried to push him into the moat.

"Isn't it clear?" Zenta said. "You pointed out earlier that the chamberlain had no legitimate standing without you. He has that standing now with Yoshiteru in his hands."

"Yoshiteru will never speak out for the chamberlain!" declared Lady Tama.

"Yoshiteru may have a knife at his back," said Zenta.

"But how can our surrender help?" asked Lady Tama with stiff lips. "It still doesn't prevent him from killing the boy when I am in his power."

"There is only one thing to do," said Zenta quietly. "Let me go out to them."

"What can you possibly do?" she cried. "You haven't a chance of rescuing him. You're just throwing your life away!"

Zenta examined her face in silence. He had already made his decision. What he was going to say was cruel, but it had to be done. "Lady Tama, since Shigeteru has been murdered, you have only one brother left. Do you want Yoshiteru killed also?"

Chapter 14

Saemon sighed. "I was pretty sure that you knew the truth. That's the reason why I could not afford to let you fall into the chamberlain's hands again. If he should learn from you that we are not retainers of the daimyo's envoy but merely a band of ronin here under false pretenses, then we shall not last half an hour, as you so unkindly put it."

"How did you find out that the envoy was really Shigeteru in disguise?" asked Lady Tama.

Zenta looked at her rueful face and smiled. "It was *your* behavior more than anything else. Your grief at his murder was the grief for a lost brother."

"That couldn't have been the only reason why you were suspicious," said Lady Tama.

"No, it was during the dinner party on the night I arrived when I first suspected the envoy was not what he seemed," said Zenta. "I was curious to find out how well he was acquainted with Lord Okudaira, and I mentioned the famous poetry party where the men improvised verses all night to *Ono no Komachi*, the legendary ninth century beauty. To my complete astonishment, the 'envoy' put me in my place for presuming to gossip about my betters."

Matsuzo suddenly remembered the envoy's rebuke during the dinner party, and Zenta's startled reaction. He knew now that it was not humiliation, but the surprising discovery about the envoy that had shocked Zenta into dropping his chopsticks.

"I think the 'envoy' was trying to change the subject," continued Zenta. "But it showed that he thought I was talking about your father's current love affairs. Then I knew that he had not been with Lord Okudaira as he had claimed. To devise a further test, I asked him about the daimyo's archery contest this spring, when the weather was so bad."

Lady Tama broke in. "But the weather was superb during the contest! I remember it perfectly!"

"Precisely. But a person who had not been there at the time could not know this. None of the castle people at dinner knew either, since they had been hired locally by the chamberlain and did their service entirely at the castle. Well, your brother fell into the trap. He agreed with me about how muddy the track was and invented a story about some illness to explain why he did not take part in the contest."

"I knew that story about the illness was a bad idea," muttered Saemon. "One should never embroider a lie."

Zenta smiled. "He had been telling a whole string of lies. Once I knew that he was lying, the rest was easy. Everyone in the region was expecting Shigeteru to return. If the envoy was really Shigeteru, it explained why he was traveling with a meager train of only forty men, and why many of the men had a raw, provincial look."

He bowed politely to Saemon. "I don't mean you, of course."

"Shigeteru told me that you were looking at him rather strangely," said Saemon. "That's why he wanted to have a private talk with you. If it turned out that you knew our secret, he was going to try to get you on our side. But someone killed him before he had a chance to see you again."

Zenta nodded. "The chamberlain suspected that I had information about Shigeteru. In fact he thought for a while that *I* was Shigeteru. I may still be able to use this fact to our advantage."

"What do you mean to do?" asked Lady Tama in alarm. "Of course we can't let you go back to the chamberlain with our secret."

"Yoshiteru's safety is more important than your secret," said Zenta. "Don't you realize that if you lose this brother also, then the command of this castle will pass away from your family altogether? That is, unless you marry the chamberlain. And you refuse to do that."

"I don't have to marry the chamberlain in order to become mistress of this castle!" said Lady Tama angrily. "There are other men I can marry."

Zenta's eyes were stern. "Do you really want to become mistress of the castle at the expense of your brother's life?"

Lady Tama stared back at him. Then slowly her eyes filled with tears. She lowered her head and finally said with a catch, "No, you are right. You must go and attempt to rescue Yoshiteru."

"Let me go with you," Matsuzo said to Zenta.

"No," said Zenta. "If you accompany me, the chamberlain will be more wary and tighten his precautions around Yoshiteru."

From the windows of the outer fortress, they watched him slowly make his way to the waiting group. He had the careful walk of a man who was conserving his strength.

Down by the moat the chamberlain broke into a smile of pure delight when he recognized the approaching figure.

Zenta soon found that the press of men around him prevented him from getting any closer. He raised his voice. "I have been sent by Lady Tama to negotiate."

As the report of what he said was carried down, a path opened in front of him. On the other three sides, the chamberlain's men were careful to press close.

Zenta pushed forward until he was within ten feet of the chamberlain. From that point on naked swords blocked his way.

"That's close enough!" cried the chamberlain nervously. "Now tell me what Lady Tama has to say."

"I have been instructed to say that in exchange for releasing Yoshiteru to her, Lady Tama will persuade the envoy's men to withdraw their accusation that you murdered their master," Zenta announced.

Jihei and the chamberlain exchanged looks. After a moment the latter said, "I refuse to bargain with Yoshiteru's life. However, if Lady Tama and the envoy's men will step down from their ridiculous position in the outer fortress, I myself will prove that I am innocent of the murder."

Zenta pretended to think over the proposal. Then he nodded. "Actually, this is what I have been trying to tell them. For all her beauty, Lady Tama sometimes acts like a spoiled child."

There was a stir among the men. It was possible that the men of the castle didn't like to hear a member of their lord's family criticized by a stranger.

Zenta turned as if to leave. "Shall I return and tell them that this is your final word?"

"Wait, don't go yet," said the chamberlain with heavy friendliness. "Stay a while. There are still a few things I want to discuss with you."

Zenta paused. "Yes, it would be pointless to return. I've known for some time that the position of Lady Tama and her supporters is hopeless."

At this statement there was a faint sound from Yoshiteru, and the woman holding him tightened her grip. Zenta refused to meet the boy's eyes.

The chamberlain beamed. Things were turning out better than he had expected. "As I have told you before, it can be quite rewarding to cooperate with me," he said cordially. "After you have proved your loyalty, you will find it a very good life."

Zenta nodded as if he had come to a decision. "Then I will prove my loyalty right now." He lowered his voice slightly. "I have some urgent information about Shigeteru which you should know immediately."

Jihei gave a start. He thrust himself forward in order to hear more clearly.

Zenta looked at him with narrowed eyes. Turning back to the chamberlain he said, "Are you sure that you want everybody to hear?" He jerked his head to indicate Jihei.

The chamberlain considered. "Very well," he said and commanded the crowd to step back. Then he signed for Zenta to approach closer.

Jihei tried to catch his master's eye. "Wait, I don't think it's safe . . ."

"Step back," ordered the chamberlain and glared suspiciously at his henchman. He had his own way of taking precaution, however. Seizing Yoshiteru, he placed the boy in front of him as a shield. The woman held tightly to the boy's other arm.

Yoshiteru wriggled in the painful grip. He looked up at Zenta with desperate appeal. "They locked up my mother, and when our fighting women tried to protect us, these men killed them!" he cried.

"My men have been waiting for a long time to get rid of those three fiends with their halberds," laughed the chamberlain.

Zenta thought of the women warriors who had helped him so generously during the ghost hunt. He remembered their fierce courage, their irrepressible humor and their exuberance with the halberd.

The chamberlain must have seen a dangerous look in Zenta's face, for he retreated a step, holding Yoshiteru even more tightly. The boy suddenly lifted his foot and kicked back as hard as he could. The chamberlain yelped and dropped his hands. Yoshiteru promptly threw himself forward.

That was all Zenta needed. Ignoring the violent stab of pain in his shoulder, he whipped his sword up with both hands and brought it down and across with all his strength. The fantastic blade went through the woman's neck and cut into the chamberlain's chest with one continuous motion. The chamberlain gave a choked cry, then fell and lay still.

Yoshiteru whimpered a little when the blood cascaded down his back. Then he drew a great shuddering breath and held himself erect. His resemblance to Lady Tama was never more obvious.

Some of the men started forward, but they retreated again at the sight of Zenta's dripping sword. He addressed them before anyone could speak. "The chamberlain was a faithless vassal who threatened the lives of his lord's family. He deserved to die."

There was some murmuring, but no one moved.

Then Jihei strode forward. "Do you call yourselves samurai?" he cried to the motionless crowd. "Will no one lift a hand to avenge his master?"

"Your master is here: Yoshiteru," said Zenta quickly. "If anyone lifts his hand and raises his weapon, he makes himself an outcast from this castle and a ronin."

"You are a ronin yourself and an intruder to our castle," returned Jihei. He turned to the men around him. "Are you going to stand there listening while your master lies dead at your feet?"

Still no one moved. In the flickering torchlight, the men stood as motionless as wooden statues in a temple.

"Then *I* shall have to teach you how a true samurai acts," said Jihei and drew his sword.

As Zenta watched Jihei's massive figure

approach, he knew that it would be a miracle if he survived more than three passes with his opponent. He stared at the set of the heavy shoulders, calculating just how the blow would come. In the end it was instinct rather than conscious will that moved his body out of the way and brought his sword up for the return blow. But his movements were tardy, and the effort cost him more than he could afford.

Jihei was puzzled. He couldn't understand why his opponent held his sword so awkwardly, or why the riposte was so feeble. Knowing the other man's caliber, he suspected a trick. Cautiously, he retreated a step.

Zenta moved a little to the left. He didn't want the light from the nearest torchbearer to fall on the blood that was rapidly spreading over the upper part of his kimono. In raising his sword to strike at the chamberlain, he had displaced the bandage on his shoulder and started the wound bleeding again. He knew he had to finish the fight before he lost too much blood. Some of the spectators noticed his condition, and there was a low buzz of whispering.

Jihei took a deep breath and lunged forward again, swinging a powerful wheel stroke, followed by a lightning fast remise. This time Zenta was forced to parry. He twisted his blade sharply to avoid the full force of the blow. Nevertheless the impact sent fire coursing through his left shoulder, and he stifled a gasp.

They had shifted ground after the exchange. Now for the first time, Jihei saw Zenta fully illuminated by the torches. His eyes took in the red stain, and he finally understood the reason for his opponent's weakness. He knew that he had the other man completely at his mercy.

Zenta swayed. He closed his eyes and sank down on one knee. Jihei approached slowly, in no hurry to give the finishing stroke. He wanted time to enjoy his triumph.

As Jihei, smiling contentedly, closed in for the death blow, Zenta's sword flashed up from the ground in a low, vicious arc. It struck his opponent's legs with all the force and speed produced by ten years of single-minded training. To the spectators, it seemed that both men went down together.

After an eternity, Zenta got slowly to his feet and looked down at the big man on the sandy ground. With the tendons of both legs cut through, Jihei struggled without success to rise. His breath hissed and he collapsed back.

"Bind up his legs and stop his bleeding," ordered Zenta, "so that he will be able to commit hara-kiri."

Jihei deserved the privilege of hara-kiri. He was a brave man and a loyal one in his own way.

Then Zenta looked around dizzily, seeking Yoshiteru. The boy tore himself from the edge of the crowd and ran up eagerly. Zenta put his arms around the small shoulders. Only the men who were very close to them could tell that he was leaning on the boy for support.

"Here is your rightful feudal lord," Zenta told the silent crowd. "Get down on your knees and swear allegiance to him."

Chapter 15

"Of course, it's unseemly to have a full-scale celebration with the dead still lying uncremated," said Ume. "But considering the magnitude of our victory, the men are having some saké in the dining hall. Saemon thought this would be a good opportunity to establish a friendly understanding between his men and the castle samurai."

It was the next morning, and Ume was describing the impromptu victory party that was taking place in the dining hall. Lady Tama, far from opposing the idea, had enthusiastically given orders for the cooks to get busy. Naturally, Zenta and Matsuzo were expected as guests of honor.

"Where is Lady Tama now?" asked Zenta. He was sitting listlessly on the floor of their room, and looked up only briefly when Ume entered.

"She is in her own room, wild with frustration at not being able to join a men's party. I told her that since we are no longer in a state of emergency, she must observe decorum once again, as befitting the mistress of this castle." Ume laid particular emphasis on her last words, and looked challengingly at Zenta.

He merely nodded indifferently and said, "I think I'll stay in my room also. I want to get some rest."

"What?" cried Ume. "But there will be plenty of good food!"

"I simply don't feel like a party," said Zenta curtly.

At the door, Ume turned and whispered to Matsuzo, "He must be sicker than he looks if he refuses food. Perhaps his wound is making him feverish."

Matsuzo was worried about Zenta, too. He had watched the physician bandage the wound, and he had seen that it was merely a flesh wound, unlikely to cause complications. Loss of blood alone couldn't account for the present low spirits.

"Why don't you join the party?" Zenta asked the younger man after Ume had left.

"There is something on your mind, isn't there?" said Matsuzo. "Perhaps I can help."

Zenta opened his eyes and considered the younger man for a moment. "Maybe you can," he said slowly. But before he could go on, the door opened to admit Saemon.

The man who had acted with equal success both as an envoy's chief retainer and as the leader of an insurrection now entered the room with a firm and confident step. He thanked Zenta warmly for his help and expressed his admiration for the way he had handled matters.

Then he said, "You know, Lady Tama is not altogether pleased at the way you took it on yourself to proclaim Yoshiteru lord of the castle."

"Why not?" asked Zenta. "Does she object to seeing her brother proclaimed?"

Saemon's admiration for Lady Tama apparently stopped short of infatuation. He took the time to consider the question objectively. "I think she is willing to accept him as lord of the castle. With Shigeteru dead, who else is there? But she wants the initiative to come from herself, so that all the control doesn't pass to the boy's mother."

"Lady Kaede doesn't have a single supporter," Zenta pointed out.

Saemon looked at him curiously. "Then you don't count yourself as one? You must know that most of the castle men would follow your lead. Part of Lady Tama's fear is that your support for Yoshiteru is the result of your feelings towards his mother. Lady Tama hates her stepmother."

When Zenta made no answer, Saemon didn't pursue the subject. After a pause he said, "Now that Shigeteru's murder has been avenged, my business here is really finished. I am a ronin, just as you are. Perhaps we can join forces." Then he gave a little laugh. "I might even give up my wandering life and settle down. Would you enter Lady Tama's service if she wanted you?"

Zenta gave a noncommittal grunt and said,

"How long have you known that your friend was Okudaira Shigeteru? He kept quiet about it until he received news of Lord Okudaira's death, I suppose."

"That's right," said Saemon. "How did you guess? We had known each other for three years, and he never gave a hint!"

"He was a clever man, and very brave," murmured Zenta. One might disapprove of the dead man, but one had to give him credit for sheer nerve.

"Yes, he was full of ideas," said Saemon, reminiscing. "Why, there was the time when he pretended . . ." He broke off when he saw that Zenta had leaned back and closed his eyes. "Are you all right? Shall I call the physician again?" he asked in concern.

Matsuzo, who was getting to know his friend pretty well, suddenly realized that Zenta was as tense as a drawn bow and was feverishly waiting for Saemon to leave. He said, "I think Zenta just needs a good rest. No doubt by tomorrow morning, he will be cheerfully discussing plans for the future."

Saemon immediately apologized for disturbing them. He repeated his expressions of gratitude and quickly left the room.

After the door closed Zenta lay perfectly still. Matsuzo regarded him for a while and then asked quietly, "What are you planning to do?"

"See if there is anyone in the corridor," ordered Zenta.

Matsuzo carefully slid the door open and put his head out. "There is no one," he reported.

Zenta got up and leaned against a pillar until his head cleared. Then he picked up his swords. "Let's go."

They walked quietly down the hall. Turning a corner, they came face to face with the little maid, who was bringing them trays of food.

"I-I thought y-you were resting in your room," she stammered.

Zenta frowned. "I'm looking for the privy. May I have your gracious permission to go?" he asked icily.

She reddened, pointed out the direction to them and fled. In her confusion she didn't ask herself why a man looking for the privy should go completely armed.

They were able to find their way to the envoy's room without further encounters.

The guards in front of the envoy's room were surprised to see the two men, but they bowed with extreme respect. They had witnessed Zenta's duel with Jihei, and they knew he was high in Saemon's esteem. When he asked to enter the envoy's room to pay his respects privately to the dead man, they didn't think of questioning him. Opening the door, they bowed once more and stood back to let the two men enter.

When the door closed, Zenta's eyes went to the envoy's body. It was carefully arranged on a mattress and covered by a quilt. Instead of approaching the body, however, he went to the stained patch on the tatami mat where the body had been discovered. Some attempt had been made to wipe the blood, but it had soaked deeply into the reed cover and the stain was still visible.

Zenta bent down to lift the corner of one mat. He winced and said, "Help me with this."

Matsuzo took another corner and together they lifted the tatami mat and then another one and a third. A path was opened from the site of the body to the emergency exit in the corner of the room.

Clearly printed on the bare wooden floor under the mats was a series of footprints. The blood had dried, and the prints were now dark brown.

They stared in silence. Finally Matsuzo spoke. "So that was how the murderer escaped from the room without leaving another visible footprint! He simply lifted each tatami mat, stood it on its side and walked on the bare floor. Then he replaced the mat behind him! How did you guess that this was the trick?"

"I remembered the ghost hunt, when Jihei's men broke into Lady Tama's rooms and lifted the mats one by one, trying to find hidden equipment for the ghost. I realized that the tatami could hide footprints as well."

After a moment Matsuzo said, "I still don't see why the murderer didn't just walk normally to the escape hole. Why did he go to the trouble of hiding his footprints?"

Even as the words left his mouth, Matsuzo saw the answer. "I see. These prints are those of a woman. The murderess wanted the blame to fall on us or on one of Jihei's men. Who is she?"

Zenta didn't answer, but the torment on his face was plain to see. He turned slowly to the door and said, "I am going to talk to her."

Matsuzo made a move to follow, but Zenta said sharply, "No! I am going alone."

As Zenta made his way to Lady Kaede's apartments, he had no premonition of danger. He wanted desperately to find frankness, not treachery. He remembered Yoshiteru's laughing face at their first meeting, and hoped that the boy was still asleep.

A group of terrified ladies met him at the entrance to Lady Kaede's rooms. They had already suffered two invasions in the last two days. The invasion of the ghost hunters had been annoying, but there had been amusing moments. The second invasion had been harrowing. The women fighters had been slaughtered and Yoshiteru dragged out screaming. Now, the mere sight of an armed man was enough to start them twittering with fear.

They quieted at last when they recognized him as their young master's rescuer. Even his request for a private interview with their mistress caused only a mild ripple of shock.

Lady Kaede was in the same reception room

as before, but this time she was arranging flowers. Her incredibly small and slender hands were more beautiful than the blossoms they held.

"It seems that once more I am to thank you for saving the life of my son," she murmured.

Without any preamble Zenta said, "I was in the envoy's room, and I saw the footprints under the tatami mats."

For five hundred years the women in Lady Kaede's family had been trained to hide their feelings. With absolute calm she said, "I don't understand. Why are you telling me about the footprints?"

"Those footprints were incriminating because it's obvious that they were made by a woman. That was why they were hidden under the tatami mats."

The flowers fell from her hands, but her beautiful eyes regarded him steadily. "What you are saying, then, is that the murder of the envoy was committed by a woman. There are many women in this castle working for the chamberlain. One of them could have done the deed."

"The chamberlain hated the envoy, but he knew better than to try to murder him. The chamberlain would be blamed for the murder, and that would be the end of his hopes for succeeding Lord Okudaira."

Her glance did not falter, but she shifted her tactics. "Tama is a girl of strong emotions. Perhaps she was in love with the envoy,

162

and he repulsed her advances."

"Lady Kaede," said Zenta softly, "let us stop pretending. The envoy was Lady Tama's brother in disguise, and you knew this perfectly well. You and I were the only two people in the dining hall who knew that the envoy had made a slip. The castle samurai who were present did not go to the daimyo's capital because they were the chamberlain's men, hired to serve him here. But you knew about the poetry party and the archery contest because you had accompanied Lord Okudaira."

She lifted a hand to brush a flower petal from her lap, but otherwise she sat motionless. Her perfume, which had intoxicated him earlier, now nauseated him.

Dropping his voice to a whisper, Zenta continued. "Those footprints were made by very small feet. Not only were they too small to be a man's, but only centuries of inbreeding could produce the fine bones which made those prints."

He suddenly reached over and plucked her dagger from her sash, the dagger which all women of her class wore. She did not even flinch from his touch.

"Washed clean, of course," he murmured. "But you are not an expert at cleaning weapons, and you have left some minute traces of blood in the ornamental work."

He was hoping she would claim that she had acted in a panic, that she had killed the envoy to protect her son. But she retained a cold control which seemed monstrous when compared to Lady Tama's hot-blooded impulsiveness.

Now that denial was useless, she talked about the murder quite willingly. "Shigeteru had to die, of course. I killed him secretly so that the chamberlain wouldn't know. If he found out that Shigeteru was no longer a threat, he would feel free to kill my son and marry Tama."

"But why were you so ready to regard Shigeteru as an enemy?" he cried. "He and Yoshiteru were brothers, and they might have come to love each other!"

"Never!" she said, and her enmity was completely unyielding. "Shigeteru and Yoshiteru were only half brothers. They could never be friends. Shigeteru was an enemy, and Tama will always be an enemy."

A wave of hopelessness swept over him. She was the most beautiful woman he had ever met, and she was a murderess. He knew with certainty that if she were allowed to rule the castle in Yoshiteru's name, Lady Tama's life would not be safe.

She looked at him contemptuously. "Why do I have to listen to you? You are only a penniless ronin, and you have no right to meddle in the affairs of this castle."

"You are wrong," he said slowly. "I have earned the right to protect Lady Tama from assassination and the right to insure that

Yoshiteru grows up to be a true samurai, not something crooked and warped that murders in secret."

She stared at him wordlessly. Then slowly she grew very pale. With a great effort she found her voice. "What do you want me to do?"

Despite everything Zenta was filled with admiration for her courage. But he had to harden himself. "There is only one thing for you to do: Cut off your hair and enter a nunnery," he said, handing her the dagger.

Slowly, as if in a trance, she reached for the dagger. "But what about my son?" she asked. "Tama will take her revenge on him if she learns that I killed the envoy."

"I promise not to tell her the truth if you leave for the nunnery immediately."

She gazed at the dagger and was silent. Then she raised her head and looked at him proudly. "Very well, I will leave now. You alone shall accompany me. I know of a nunnery a few miles from here."

"Don't you want to see Yoshiteru and say good-bye to him?"

"No, I don't think I can face his tears," she replied with a bitter smile. "It's much better to leave like this. You and Tama can tell him whatever you wish when I am gone."

Zenta nodded assent. He could understand her feelings. A farewell scene between mother and son would be unbearable.

She summoned an attendant. "Bring me

165

traveling sandals and a veil. I am going to the family temple to pray in front of my husband's tomb."

The attendant obeyed this sudden order without question. The recent shocking events had left her no room for further surprise.

As Zenta followed Lady Kaede down the wooden walk and across the courtyard, he felt like an executioner walking behind his victim. Passing through the fortress on their way out, they met some men who recognized Zenta. They glanced curiously at his veiled female companion. One or two of the men started to call out friendly greetings, but faltered when they saw his expression. It did not encourage conversation.

They walked along the moat until they were out of sight of the guards at the gate. Suddenly Lady Kaede seemed to stumble. "Please stop," she gasped. "I feel a little faint."

Still under the spell of her beauty, Zenta forgot caution. He reached over to support her swaying figure. Her dagger flashed out, faster than a striking serpent.

There was a sudden sound of running. Her hand hesitated for a fraction of a second, and that saved his life. He flung up his arm to ward off the blow, and the dagger ripped harmlessly into his sleeve.

Lady Tama was running towards them, her eyes blazing with fury. "You murderess!" she screamed. "You're trying to kill again!"

Faced with her most implacable enemy, Lady Kaede realized at last that there was no hope. She dropped the dagger and began to retreat. Lady Tama continued to advance. Her face had the inhuman look of an avenging deity. Step by step Lady Kaede moved back until she was at the very edge of the moat.

Then without a word she suddenly turned and flung herself into the moat. The impact of her body parted the water so that it resembled the mouth of a monster swallowing its prey.

Zenta rushed to the edge and leaned over the moat. But Lady Tama held him back, digging her fingers into his wounded shoulder until he gasped with pain.

"No!" she cried. "Stand back. It's better this way."

After a minute they turned away, unable to watch the struggles in the dark water below.

Zenta finally looked at Lady Tama's white face beside him. "You saved my life. How did you get here at just the right moment?"

"Ume was bringing food to the guards at Shigeteru's room and they told her about the footprints. As soon as she saw the prints, she was struck by their small size. She came and told me. I rushed over to Kaede's rooms, and the servants told me you had come this way."

Zenta drew a shaky breath. "Now I understand how she managed to catch the envoy off guard and kill him." He looked back briefly at the now quiet moat. "You knew her much better than I did. I was a blind fool."

Generosity was Lady Tama's most endearing trait. She could have said, "You thought I hated my stepmother solely because of jealousy." But instead she said, "She deceived my father, too. She was a very beautiful woman."

They turned away from the moat and started back for the inner courtyard. "I shall have to break the news to Yoshiteru," Zenta said heavily.

"It's really my job, too," said Lady Tama. "I'll come with you."

When Yoshiteru's tousled head appeared, the first thing he asked was, "Where is my mother?"

Then he caught sight of his sister and he broke into a wide grin. "Tama! What a pleasant surprise! You don't come here very often."

When he saw Zenta, too, his delight was complete. The two people he admired most had come to visit him. "Since we have company, we ought to have refreshments," he said gleefully. "I even remember which kind of confection you like best."

Zenta was watching Lady Tama, his heart in his mouth. She stared at her brother silently, and her expression was impossible to read. The silence seemed to drag on and on.

Yoshiteru glanced from one to the other, looking very puzzled. Finally he said in an uncertain tone, "I'd like to have refreshments brought for our party, but I don't know whom to call. Everyone seems to be gone."

Suddenly Lady Tama ran over to her young brother and caught him fiercely to her. He squealed a little in protest at her tight embrace, but then resigned himself. After all, women were such emotional creatures!

"Yoshiteru, your mother is very ill," Lady Tama said huskily. "But don't worry, I'm here to take care of you."

Chapter 16

Lady Tama's feelings were deeply hurt. She was in her music room, where the mellow afternoon light shone on various instruments and books lying about. The clutter had not been improved by the ransacking of the ghost hunters. She looked reproachfully at Zenta and Matsuzo, who were seated before her. They had come to say farewell.

"I don't understand you!" Lady Tama said to Zenta. "Why do you insist on leaving now? Can't you at least wait until your shoulder has healed?"

Zenta looked stubborn. "This kind of settled life doesn't suit me. I would soon get restless."

"But there is work for you here," she insisted. "Just think of all the vacancies that you've created in our staff."

"You don't need me. There are plenty of good men here." Zenta's voice was expressionless, and it made him sound cold.

Matsuzo was surprised at Zenta's coldness. He could see that Lady Tama was swallowing her pride and almost begging them to stay.

She made an obvious effort to control her temper. "You came looking for a job, and I can offer you any position you wish. Then why do you wish to leave?"

When Zenta didn't answer, she struck at a zither viciously, making harsh, jangling chords. Then she said in a low voice, "Are you afraid that Yoshiteru will hear about your part in his mother's death? You know that I will never tell him the truth. I plan to announce that my step-mother has retired to a nunnery for religious reasons. In due course her death from illness will be announced. My brother will not have any cause to hate you."

"That's not the reason why I'm leaving," said Zenta. For a moment he seemed about to add something, but he remained silent.

"My brother and I will need someone to pro-tect us from evil men like the chamberlain," Lady Tama pleaded. "You're forgetting that Yoshiteru is only nine years old. Until he be-comes of age, I have to direct things alone. What if the daimyo really sends an envoy here, someone who might dispute the succession?"

"You know very well that the daimyo was fully prepared to recognize Yoshiteru as heir," Zenta reminded her. "He never had any inten-tion of sending an envoy. All the doubts about Yoshiteru were raised by the chamberlain and the false envoy."

"But I need a new chamberlain, and I need someone to command the armed men if the daimyo should send for a levy," said Lady Tama. "I'm planning to recall my father's old retainers from the outlying forts, and for these veterans I need a seasoned commander."

"Yoshiteru will come of age in six years. Until then you have Saemon. He is both courageous and resourceful."

"Saemon?" she said. "But he was Shigeteru's man. He might not want to serve Yoshiteru."

Zenta gave a sigh of exasperation. "Lady Tama, Saemon was not Shigeteru's follower. He was a ronin, an adventurer whom your brother met on his travels. The two of them probably made their plans together. With matters turning out this way, Saemon would be glad to accept a job here."

As Lady Tama still looked dubious, Zenta said, "I don't know what stories Ume has been telling you, but Shigeteru was not a young aristocrat traveling with a retinue of devoted followers. He was sent alone from the castle into exile, a punishment which he fully deserved."

She sprang up in a fury. "How dare you talk about my brother like that!"

Ignoring her outburst Zenta went on. "Your brother, the only one left, is Yoshiteru. He has his mother's courage and his father's high sense of honor. He deserves all your love and support. Don't waste time sorrowing for Shigeteru. He wasn't worth it."

Matsuzo held his breath. He himself had felt a certain dislike for the dead envoy, but he would never have risked Lady Tama's anger by speaking out like this. For a moment he expected her to summon guards and order their immediate punishment.

Instead of calling her guards, however, she broke into a storm of weeping. Perhaps she was remembering the help that Zenta had given—disinterested help, because he had asked for no reward.

Matsuzo glanced at Zenta and found his expression grave, with an undercurrent of sadness.

Finally Lady Tama raised her eyes, and in a voice choked with sobs she said, "Go, then. I don't ever want to see you again!"

She wiped her eyes and struck blindly at her zither. As the two men walked out of the room, the music, fast and furious, sounded in waves behind their backs.

On their way through the inner courtyard, Matsuzo looked around at the beautifully landscaped grounds, now peaceful and quiet. He sighed wistfully. "It's actually rather pleasant here."

Zenta stopped. "Why don't you stay, then?" he asked. "Lady Tama would be glad to offer you a good position."

"No, I don't really want to stay," said Matsuzo. "It will be quiet and dull here when you're gone. I'd rather go with you and get into more adventures."

"Get into more adventures? Into more trouble, you mean. I hope you realize that your chances of dying peacefully in bed will be poor if you go with me."

Upon leaving the women's quarters, Zenta

did not go to the main gate. Instead he went in the opposite direction.

Matsuzo was puzzled. "This is not the way out. We came in the other way."

"I know. There's a little back gate where the inner moat branches out to join the outer moat. I want to go that way to avoid meeting a lot of people and having to answer questions."

But there was no gate at the place Zenta described.

After staring blankly at the unbroken wall for a moment, he muttered, "I must have made a mistake. Come on, let's go out by the main gate, then."

A suspicion began to grow in Matsuzo. He suddenly remembered other inconsistencies in his friend's behavior. For example, there was Zenta's attitude toward Lady Tama. Although he seemed to feel a deep affection for her, he showed none of the awe that was due to a lady of beauty, spirit, and high rank.

At the gate, just as expected, they were surrounded by curious guards. The castle men did not presume to detain the two ronin against their will, but they wanted to know the reason for their sudden departure.

While Zenta dealt curtly with the questions, Matsuzo drew one of the guards aside and asked quietly, "Was there formerly a back gate at the place where the inner moat branches out?"

"I don't believe so," answered the man.

"Yes, there was one," said a second man who had overheard them. "But Lord Okudaira ordered it taken out so that there would be fewer exits to defend. That happened eight years ago."

Eventually Zenta managed to brush aside the rest of the questions, and they were free to go. They passed silently through the last gate and across the bridge over the outer moat. As the gate clanged shut behind them, Matsuzo couldn't contain himself any longer. "You couldn't possibly have known about the back gate unless you used to live here," he said at last.

Zenta became still. He made no reply.

"This would also explain how you knew the castle so well," Matsuzo went on. "When we were running around during the ghost hunt and afterwards during our escape, you never had trouble finding your way in those mazelike corridors."

Zenta looked at Matsuzo's face and realized that denial was useless. "I gave myself away when I mentioned the back gate, didn't I? It's fortunate that I didn't make that slip while Jihei was around."

Matsuzo shook his head in bewilderment. "I still don't see why Ume didn't recognize you."

"Why should she? She was so convinced that the false envoy was the long lost son that she was blind to anyone else."

Matsuzo nodded. He remembered the old woman saying that when Shigeteru left the castle, he was still an immature youth. In the

175

last ten years he had grown much taller. His face had lost the fullness of youth and grown thin with hardships. But the chief factor must have been psychological. Ume found it easy to believe that her aristocratic young master would return in the guise of a well-dressed envoy at the head of forty men. She would never believe that he could appear in the form of a half-starved ronin wearing a torn kimono.

"When did you decide to come back to the castle?" asked Matsuzo.

"I had heard rumors about Shigeteru's return, and I suspected that someone was planning to impersonate me. He was a clever man, whoever he was. By secretly telling Tama that he was not a real envoy, he appealed to her romantic nature. He knew she would be only too eager to believe that he was her long lost brother. I couldn't let an impostor take control here, especially since he might harm Yoshiteru."

"Now that the false envoy and the chamberlain are both dead, why didn't you take command?" asked Matsuzo, feeling a keen regret. "What made you change your mind about claiming the succession? Lady Tama and the castle men would be overjoyed if you came forward."

"But I never had any intention of claiming the succession!" cried the other man. He was silent for a moment, and then said in a low voice, "Ten years ago, I accused my father of cowardice. I was talking wildly, but he was too hurt and too proud to defend his action. After I had already left the castle, I learned that my father had retreated because he was obeying the daimyo's battle orders." The set of his bloodless lips revealed how much pain the admission was costing him.

"I received news this May that my father was seriously ill. I went to the daimyo's capital during the archery contest in order to steal a look at him. He looked so old and frail! I knew then that I had broken my father's heart when I accused him of cowardice."

"But your error was a perfectly natural one!"

"No! It was unforgivable! I lost my right to the succession forever. Now that my job here is finished, I have no reason to stay any longer."

Almost to himself he added softly, "By helping Yoshiteru and Tama when they were in danger, I lightened the burden of guilt that I have been carrying for the last ten years. Perhaps I can make something of my life from now on."

The restlessness that had driven him from one job to another had been the result of guilt. There was a new look of peace about him as he faced the road ahead. Matsuzo had to hurry to catch up.

They entered the pine grove, which gave out a dry tangy smell of autumn. Behind them, the serpentine walls of the castle loomed dazzling white in the sun.

Bibliography

Dorson, Richard M. *Folk Legends of Japan*. Tokyo: Tuttle, 1962.

Dunn, Charles J. *Everyday Life in Traditional Japan*. Tokyo: Tuttle, 1969.

Duus, Peter. *Feudalism in Japan*. New York: Knopf, 1969.

Frederic, Louis. *Daily Life in Japan at the Time of the Samurai*. New York: Praeger, 1972.

Fujioka, Michio. *Japanese Art in Color*, Vol. 12: *Shiro to Shoin (Castles and Residential Quarters)*. Tokyo: Shogakkan, 1968.

Hearn, Lafcadio. *In Ghostly Japan*. Tokyo: Tuttle, 1971.

———. *Kwaidan*. Tokyo: Tuttle, 1972.

Japan Times Ltd. *Japanese Castles*. Tokyo: Japan Times Photo Books Ser., 1971.

Joya, Mock. *Things Japanese*. Tokyo: Japan Publications, 1971.

McCullough, Helen C. *Yoshitsune: A 15th Century Japanese Chronicle*. Stanford University Press, 1966.

Mainichi Newspapers. *A Pageant of the Castles of Japan*. Tokyo: Mainichi, 1970.

Mitford, A. B. *Tales of Old Japan*. Tokyo: Tuttle, 1966.

Morse, Edward S. *Japanese Homes and Their Surroundings*. Tokyo: Tuttle, 1972.

Nitobe, Inazo Ota. *Bushido: the Soul of Japan; An Exposition of Japanese Thought*. Tokyo: Tuttle, 1969.

Sansom, George Bailey. *A History of Japan*, Vol. 2. London: Cresset, 1961.

Smith, Bradley. *Japan: A History in Art*. Tokyo: Gemini, 1964.

Varley, H. Paul, with Ivan and Nobuko Morris. *The Samurai*. London: The Trinity Press, 1970.

Yumoto, John M. *Samurai Sword: A Handbook*. Tokyo: Tuttle, 1958.